A CLOUDY COVER

"Sounds messy," Driver agreed. "You know damn well what the President's first question is going to be. He's going to want to know what we have to gain by putting our tit in this wringer."

It was the question Barrows had been waiting for. "Tell him everything points to the fact that the Chinese have been building and testing some type of nuclear device in the area. Less than a month ago the Swiss Seismological people in Zurich reported recording an underground nuclear explosion in that very area. Our best information up until recently has led us to believe that the Chinese closed down their Zijin Mountain base at Kamanchu several years ago. But the detonation of some sort of nuclear device in that region makes us think maybe they have reactivated it."

"And that they have built their facility in the side of the mountain so that we can't get pictures of it," his assistant added. "The way we see it, by cooperating with the IHO, we build a little goodwill by helping the Russians discover the source of the pollution. And at the same time we use this as an opportunity to find out what the Chinese have up their sleeve. This is one of those times when the right hand doesn't necessarily have to know what the left hand is doing."

Other *Leisure* books by R. Karl Largent:
THE ASSASSIN
THE SEA
RED WIND
RED SAND
RED SKIES
BLACK DEATH
RED ICE
THE LAKE
THE PROMETHEUS PROJECT
RED TIDE
THE WITCH OF SIXKILL
ANCIENTS

RED RAIN

R. KARL LARGENT

LEISURE BOOKS  NEW YORK CITY

A LEISURE BOOK®

May 2001

Published by

Dorchester Publishing Co., Inc.
276 Fifth Avenue
New York, NY 10001

ISBN 0-8439-4870-1

Printed in the United States of America.

Mentors & Heroes . . .
Rod Serling
John D. MacDonald
Lawrence Sanders

RED RAIN

Chapter One

Kamanchu Weapons Facility
Northern Mongolia
1-1

Delays irritated Wuxi Bo Lea, and the train for Ulan Bator was well over two hours late leaving the station at Kamanchu. First, there had been the lengthy and tedious inspection of travel orders and baggage conducted by a young PRK officer, the thoroughness of which made it obvious the man regarded everyone aboard the train as a potential miscreant. Then there was a further delay when, as Wuxi was informed, a work detail was dispatched ahead of the train to clear the tracks of boulders and debris resulting from the recent rash of earth tremors in the region.

True, the total departure from schedule amounted to less than three hours, but it was impinging on what little time he had allowed himself for sight-seeing in the capital city. The next morning his flight left for Beijing.

Now, as he was feeling the first feeble lurches of the train car and the grating sound of steel wheels against metal rails, he was finally able to settle back into his seat. He had already determined that sleep would be impossible until a raucous group of young officers in the compartment adjacent to his either drank themselves into a state of oblivion or grew tired of playing cards and sought other amusements. From the nature of their loud, frequently profane conversation it was obvious they needed a few days of leave and a chance to ventilate. Wuxi had further decided that they were collectively destined to return to the base at Kamanchu both poorer and disappointed. True, there was a seamy side to Ulan Bator, but Wuxi knew the young men were not as likely to find what they were looking for as they hoped. The city's limited nightlife, only a small handful of major hotels such as the Ulan Bator and the Bayangol, and the necessity of acquiring a taste for local beers made Wuxi certain the train ride to and from the Mongolian capital would prove the highlight of the officers' seventy-two-hour pass.

Despite the delay and the clamor in the next compartment, Wuxi viewed his own situation as fortunate. It was his last scheduled visit to Kamanchu and the

Zijin Mountain facility. Because of that he had planned a few hours of sight-seeing in Ulan Bator prior to his flight home. His admittedly flexible itinerary called for a brief visit to Sukhe Bator Square and attending the afternoon performance at the National Opera. He had inquired ahead and learned that the opera house was presenting modern operatic versions of ancient Mongolian folk tales. Because this was his last trip, he was eager to experience what he could of his host country's culture.

As the train gathered momentum and emerged from the cold concrete bowels of the mountain complex, it cleared the last vestiges of the Kamanchu facility. There was just enough daylight left for Wuxi to catch fleeting glimpses of the area's black-green forests and rolling hills. These scenes, after crossing the Jingsan Bridge, would be followed by the inevitable descent into the valley to follow the course of the Solonge. Then there would be nothing to see. With daylight fading there was already a thin coat of frost on his window.

Because Wuxi knew he would be unable to sleep until the bedlam in the next compartment subsided, he briefly considered beginning the reports he was expected to submit prior to accepting his new assignment with the Social Improvement Ministry in Beijing. As a going-away gift, Colonel Kang Lim, the facilities commander of the Zijin Mountain Project, had presented him with a rare and costly leather-bound copy of Sun Tzu's *The Art of War*. Even though Wuxi had studied it in great detail during his days as a student, he would be proud to display such a book in his own personal library. He realized that if he did read it at this point in his life, he would do so with the less passionate mind-set of middle age. On the other hand, the prospect of starting such a book now, on the train, seemed like a daunting endeavor, and he closed his eyes instead. Wuxi chose instead to reflect back on the last four years, during which he had been assigned the responsibility of conducting the twice-a-year audit of the northern Mongolian facility.

At forty-seven years of age, Dr. Wuxi Bo Lea was married with two grown children and was enjoying the fruits of many years of hard work. He lived in Beijing and, by Party standards, enjoyed a modicum of success in his career. His recent promotion to a position in the Ministry was proof of that. At one time he had held the rank of colonel in the PRK. It was because of his unique combination of military service and education that his duty during his travels to Kamanchu had been to conduct progress reviews of the Zijin weapons-development program. It was fitting, Wuxi thought, that in concert with his last scheduled visit, Colonel Kang's staff had announced they were ready to begin testing the mini-warhead housing the long-anticipated 5KA biological-weapons system.

Too, this opportunity to visit the Mongolian capital had been a surprising stroke of good fortune. He recalled Kang's last-minute decision to permit the train to make its bimonthly run despite the recent rash of earth tremors in the area.

"The risk of a misadventure is outweighed by the need to dispose of the transuranic waste," Kang had declared. Then, in a gesture that was decidedly unlike him, the colonel had granted a number of his officers three-day passes and authorized the addition of two passenger cars for the trip to Ulan Bator.

Wuxi was still reflecting on Kang's announcement when an aging car attendant knocked, opened the door to his compartment, and informed him they were approaching the Jingsan Bridge. "I trust you have your camera ready?" the old man said. "There may still be enough light to get a good picture. . . ."

Wuxi thanked the man, fumbled in his luggage for his camera, and started to wave his hand in dismissal when he realized the man was also issuing a warning.

"The train will pause briefly before it crosses the bridge to make certain the inspection crew has cleared the way," he was saying. "It will be a short delay, but, if you wish, you may step down from the train and take pictures."

Wuxi was grateful. The Jingsan Bridge was in itself a tribute to Chinese engineering. It spanned nearly a quarter of a mile over an eight-hundred-foot-deep gorge that cradled the waters of the Solonge River below the Jingsan Dam. Wuxi had heard it was one of the most beautiful places in all of northern Mongolia.

"You will not leave me if I do?" he asked with a grin.

The old man smiled back at him. "I have taken pictures many times myself," he admitted. "Where we stop, if you look, you will see a small ledge where you can get an elevated view."

Moments later, just as the old man had indicated, the train slowed and began grinding to a stop. As it did, Wuxi gathered himself, stepped from his compartment, went to the rear of the car, and stood on the shielded platform between the train's only two passenger cars. Behind him, one car back, was the massive thirty-two-wheeled, steel-reinforced carrier with lead shields that transported the weapons-grade nuclear waste destined for a dumping site in the Gobi.

When the train finally came to a complete stop, Wuxi stepped from the platform, felt the chill mountain air swirl around him, and climbed up on the ledge the attendant had mentioned. As he checked his shutter speed, he was concerned that they had arrived at the picturesque site just a little too late in the day; there was no longer enough light to obtain the kind of photographs he had hoped for. At the same time he realized that it felt as if he were still on the train and that it was still moving.

The first tremors were slight, like ill-defined shadows shuddering in a gentle breeze. Behind him, though, he could hear tiny pebbles cascading down the grade, and his thoughts turned briefly to the reports of the seismic activity that had delayed the train's departure. This time, though, there was more than just a slight agitation; the ground beneath him was actually quivering.

Within a matter of seconds there was evidence of still-stronger convulsions, and Wuxi took the precaution of bracing himself. He remembered reading that someone had described the phenomenon of an earthquake as rock formations in long-dormant granite structures taking on a life of their own.

The shuddering sensation intensified. The ledge where he stood began to protest. The din was no longer merely unsettling; it had become menacing, and before he could react, there was a cacophony of deep-throated shrieks erupting from the very ground on which he stood.

Wuxi tried to work his way down. As he did, there was just enough daylight for him to see the ground tear open. The ribbons of steel rail across the mighty bridge's expanse began to buckle and twist.

The series of preliminary tremors lasted no more than a few seconds. But quickly, their half-muted overture became a full-blown chorus of terror. Gnarled railroad spikes began popping from roadbed ties. Rails contorted and snapped, making shrapnel out of tearing granite and steel.

The huge girders on the Jingsan Bridge wrinkled first, then crumpled, and finally began tearing away from their moorings. Wuxi, who viewed the world with scientific detachment, was no longer just an observer of a terrifying phenomenon; he had become an inexorable part of it. The immensity and horror of what was unfolding became all too apparent. The ground continued to convulse, and then in an unmistakable gesture of surrender, the hulking steel bridge warped, twisted, and snapped. The tortured steel made a symphony of sounds like nothing Wuxi had ever heard before. He watched as the huge diesel engine that had pulled his train pitched sideways, then plummeted down into the canyon, wrenching its two passenger cars and the thirty-two-wheeled nuclear waste unit behind.

Any record of the disaster Wuxi Bo Lea may have momentarily envisioned was abruptly rendered impracticable, terminated by his own terrifying plunge into the same abyss.

Schweizerischer Erdbebendienst
Swiss Seismological Service
Zurich
1-2

Dr. Huldreich Dunant was elated. He put down his pipe, leaned back to cushion himself deeper in his chair, and enjoyed the moment. The continuous two-day-old flow of analog data spewing across his monitor was confirming a theory. At last he had proof. A connection. His effort had finally paid off. Two days earlier he had recorded what he was convinced was a small underground nuclear explosion in an out-of-the-way mountainous area midway between Hatgal and Zakmensk. Now he was getting verification of seismic activity in that region during the succeeding twenty-four hours, immediately south of the blast site.

The series of five analog figures, grouped in clusters, repeated. They were trailed by aggregates of five more groupings, all confirming both the magnitude and longevity of the seismic activity. What he was seeing, surely, was clear evidence of shear activity and the subsequent seismic phenomena associated with nuclear detonation.

His smile continued to broaden as each of the repeating clusters confirmed his theory. "What do you think now, my skeptical friend?" he crowed. "Is this not a graphic example of cause and effect?"

Across the room, Kekos Kocher leaned forward—his computer was networked with Dunant's—studying the images trailing across his monitor. He peered over his glasses and squinted at the data. "The explosion was recorded when?" he asked.

Dunant checked his log. "Precisely thirty-eight hours, thirty-seven minutes, twenty-one seconds ago. Shock blast duration at point 0, three minutes and nineteen seconds. All of which is recorded and archived on the EQTA system on a K-1 line."

Kocher continued to study the data. He mistrusted any assumption that could not be checked against proven previous testing.

"This time I think we have what we need," Dunant said. "With this we can tie the two occurrences together. Proximity, time, relationship—everything we need is there."

It was Kocher's nature to be skeptical. "It could be nothing more than coincidence," he cautioned.

Dunant studied the data again for several minutes before reaffirming his conviction. "No. No coincidence. Not this time. I have been tracking it closely. There has been an uncommon frequency of minor tremors in the region since the initiating event was recorded."

Kocher—himself a proponent of the theory that an underground nuclear explosion detonated at the right time and in an area conducive to seismic activity, might trigger tremors—was nevertheless cautious. "Tremors are not precursors, nor do they forecast major short-term seismological activity," he reminded his friend. "They simply indicate—"

Dunant waved him off before his colleague could finish. "Must I remind you that I read the same books and papers you do, my friend?" He laughed. "There is no need to recite chapter and verse to me. You will see that I am right when I chart and verify the relationship between the two events."

Kocher was still questioning when he turned back to his own monitor. "What was the depth of the initiating event?"

Dunant referenced his log. "Roughly eighteen hundred and fifty meters."

"Not all that deep," Kocher observed.

"Have you considered the verticality factor?" Dunant grumbled.

Kocher continued to frown as he brought up the A-67/68 satellite maps on his monitor. The area his colleague had indicated was in a vast and remote area near the Mongolian-Russian border. He traced the latitudinal and longitudinal coordinates until he located the approximate site of the detonation. When he did, his frown deepened. "There is nothing there. Who would have detonated such an underground device?"

Dunant shrugged and shook his head. He had known his colleague a long time. "Need I remind you my expertise is in the field of geophysics, not geopolitics? Who knows who would be detonating such devices? It could be the Russians. It could be the Chinese. I doubt if it is the Mongols. They have enough problems without . . ."

Kocher smiled, nodded agreement, and continued to assess the numbers on his monitor. He was well aware what the majority of his colleagues would say. One such occurrence could be written off as an anomaly, an aberration. An identical or similar occurrence, properly archived, would be necessary to inspire further study.

On the other hand, Dunant was serious about his

work. Perhaps there *was* a relationship. Could an underground nuclear explosion detonated at such a shallow depth trigger such an event? Was it possible? Were different forces involved? Different magnitudes? Most certainly these would be events that occurred at different depths. His frown continued to deepen. Like his colleague, he was a geophysicist first—but there was always that old caveat: under the right circumstances, the right conditions, and in an area conducive to transverse or shear waves . . .

He pushed himself away from his monitor, stood up, stretched, and began to fix himself a cup of tea. "Do you intend to report this incident before you have had an opportunity to validate your conclusions?"

"I do indeed," Dunant assured him.

Center for Strategic Assessment
Washington
1-3

USAF Colonel Conrad Baxter was new to his position as Chief Deputy Assessment Officer of the CSA's worldwide data-evaluation section. He was attending his first briefing while the center's director and his new CO, General Harlan Crist, introduced him to his staff. As Crist worked his way around the table, each of the staff—most of whom were Air Force officers like himself, with only a sprinkling of civilians—welcomed him. As they were introduced, they each repeated their names and gave a brief overview of their responsibilities.

Baxter was both grateful and relieved; to a member they appeared to be both credentialed and cordial, each assuring him that they would do everything possible to make his transition from his post at Travis to his new responsibility at CSA as smooth as possible. When it was his turn, even though he knew it would sound trite, he guaranteed his new staff he had no intention of altering the section's routine.

"Years ago I learned not to screw around with something if it was working. So, for the time being at least, there will be damn few changes and we'll continue the same open-door policy established by my predecessor. I'm new and I know I have a helluva lot to learn. If you uncover something you are convinced I should be aware of, get up in my face, get my attention, and make me aware of it. I can't do my job if I don't know what's going on."

There was a group nod around the table as Baxter continued to scan the faces of his underlings.

"Now," he said, "let's see if we can get me kick-started. What's on the docket today?"

Crist pointed to a young officer at the far end of the table, and Baxter nodded in his direction.

"Captain Reimers, sir," the officer began. "Asian Review Sector." Reimers had started off on the right foot; Baxter appreciated the fact that he didn't have to exhibit his lack of recall and juggle the names of his new staff. "We received a report early this morning," Reimers continued, "from the Swiss bureau in Zurich. According to the report, they recorded and documented an underground nuclear explosion near the Mongolian-Russian border."

"When?" Crist demanded.

Reimers glanced down at the report. "Three days

ago, sir. Now they are reporting that seismic activity has occurred in the same area."

Crist stood up and walked across the room to the audiovisual control panel. "Let me show you the area Captain Reimers is talking about, Colonel." Crist began punching buttons, and a large electronic multicolored display map appeared on the screen.

"If the general pleases," Baxter interrupted, "how about a little background before we get into this?"

Reimers was ready. "For the last several years, sir, the Swiss Seismological Service has been a big help to us in reporting nuclear explosions recorded by their network. Prior to the incident in question, they confirmed a May 11, 1998, detonation in a remote area near Tura in Siberia; in an equally remote area of China, June 8, 1996; and they were able to confirm that six separate nuclear tests were conducted in French Polynesia between September of 1995 and January 1996. The five 'official' nuclear power states—what we call P5, sir, as recorded by the German National Data Center—did the verification in each case. Since, we have regarded these Swiss reports as reliable."

"And who do they believe conducted this latest test?"

"They would be guessing," Reimers admitted. "But based on what we know, we have to believe it was the Chinese, sir. It's in their backyard."

"Lead me through your logic, Captain."

Reimers went to the map and began pointing. "What you're looking at here is an area that we have been scrutinizing for quite some time now. As you can see, it is an area north and west of Ulan Bator and south of Housgal Nuur. Fifteen years ago, when Mongolia was still a Chinese protectorate, the government in Beijing built a massive earthen dam on the Elygn Gol. We have been monitoring the activity there with varying degrees of intensity ever since. More recently, that surveillance has been accomplished by means of KDL satellite.

"For the colonel's background information, that particular satellite operates in a sun-synchronous, low-altitude polar orbit. The orbital period is 101 minutes and the nominal altitude is 830 kilometers."

"And exactly what have we learned, Captain?" Baxter glanced at Crist to see if he was on track.

Reimers was suddenly a bit hesitant. "Learned? Admittedly, not a great deal, sir. We do know the Chinese built the dam, and when they did, we intensified surveillance. What we saw surprised us, though. There was a flurry of construction activity some eight kilometers upriver from the dam site near the village of Kamanchu at a place called Zijin Mountain. The activity lasted approximately twenty-four months following the construction of the dam. They also built a railroad spur that connected to the main line leading down to Ulan Bator, and a runway that could accommodate large aircraft.

"Then came the earthquake, considerable damage. As luck would have it, shortly after, and before we could complete our assessment of the damage, sunspots knocked one of our satellites haywire. It wasn't until the situation was corrected that we were able to determine the full extent of the damage. What we learned was that the earthquake had pretty much set them back to ground zero. By the time we started getting true continuity again, they were tearing out the runway. Since that time there were sufficient data to suggest that they have made very little effort to repair the damage to the on-site structures."

"When exactly was this earthquake, Captain?"

Reimers paused to check his notes, "November 1992."

Baxter, a former SAC officer, had developed a cryptic communication style over the years. By nature he was a digger, long on both patience and determination. His habit, background, and training dictated that he ask questions that were both direct and curt. He wasted little time framing his questions. "What about personnel? Ground activity?"

"Since the 1992 earthquake, very little evidence of either, sir."

Baxter looked at Crist. "With the general's permission, I'd like to table this matter until I have an opportunity to review the files on this Kamanchu situation. Then, perhaps we can discuss this matter further and I can sound at least halfway intelligent."

Crist laughed. "One thing you're going to like about your staff, Connie. They come to these meetings prepared."

Officers' Club
Langley Air Force Base
1-4

"Damn it all, Clark, you look great. How long has it been?"

Clark Barrows rolled his eyes and shook his head, trying to remember the last time he had seen Conrad

Baxter. "Well, I can't tell you how long it's been, but the last time I saw you, your hair was black and you were sporting a cluster on your shirt collar instead of an eagle."

"Damn, has it been that long? Well, there is one consolation; at least I've still got hair," Baxter countered. "So, how's Mary?"

"Mary is up in the Berkshires closing up the summer place—and she's fine. When I tell her you were here, she'll be sorry she missed you."

Baxter leaned forward with both arms on the table, ignoring his drink. "Actually, I doubt if she'll miss me; it looks like I'm going to be around town for a while. I've just been assigned to the Center for Strategic Assessment over at the Pentagon. I'm replacing a man by the name of Herb Rodman. Maybe you know him."

Barrows shook his head. "Know the name, but I never met him. Good reputation, though." He took a sip of his Manhattan, set it down, took out his pipe, and began to pack it. "I heard about Polly. She was a special lady." Then he added, "I'm sorry."

Baxter looked down and bit his lip. It was still painful to talk about. "At least she didn't have to suffer long. We discovered the malignancy on a Thursday; she died the following Tuesday. Damn shame . . . in more ways than one. We were married in Baltimore and she would have loved this tour of duty in Washington."

Barrows shoved his menu aside and studied his old friend's face. Other than the thinning and graying of what had once been an impressive crop of dark wavy hair, Conrad Baxter still looked fit enough to crawl in the cockpit of an F-16. He was tall, well-muscled, still possessed penetrating brown-black eyes that Barrows had always been convinced could see straight through to a man's soul. In addition he still sported the remnants of a California tan, and there was the distinct absence of a paunch. His old friend obviously found time for and worked hard at keeping himself in shape. "I was surprised to get your call, and doubly surprised when you indicated there was a degree of urgency," Barrows admitted.

Conrad Baxter waited until his old friend finished lighting his pipe and the waiter brought a second round of drinks. "I don't know that there was anything urgent about it, Clark. First-day jitters, I guess. I was looking for a friendly face. General Crist introduced me to my staff. That was some scary shit. Here I am pushing fifty, and everyone around that damn table appears to be a minimum of ten to fifteen years younger than me—not to mention the fact that they all have degrees out the ass. Hell, I was lucky they didn't throw me out of Baylor long before I quit."

Barrows understood. He was smiling. "Wanta bet you're the only one at that table that has any experience beside sitting at a damn desk? I know Crist. Odds are he picked you to replace Rodman because he knew no one else had the balls to keep that bunch of eggheads in line."

Baxter laughed. "Now I can understand how you survived in this damn town so long. You've still got a silver tongue."

"It helps sometime to tell it like it is." Barrows laughed. "But what's this element of urgency you referred to when you called? Need an apartment?"

Baxter paused before he answered. "That's number two on my priority list. Crist tells me your agency has been monitoring the situation at a remote Chinese weapons facility near the Mongolian-Russian border called Kamanchu."

Barrows put his pipe down and looked around before he spoke. The dining room was nearly empty. "I wouldn't exactly say we've been monitoring it, Connie, at least not lately. It's probably more accurate to say we're aware of its existence and we check on it periodically." Barrows had to think for a minute. "Seven, maybe eight years ago that area was getting a great deal of attention from damn near every agency in Washington. G7 was in charge of spearheading the effort. We even went to the trouble of putting one of our people in Ulan Bator to keep tabs on the situation. Nothing came of it, though. As I recall, there was an earthquake and whatever the PRK had in mind, they must have had second thoughts. For the most part, activity died out, and there hasn't been much going on there since. It's curious that you bring it up, though, because while it isn't Kamanchu, we have been keeping our eye on a Russian facility just north of there in the Lake Baykal area. The Russians have been testing some rather sophisticated aircraft there for the last twenty-four months. When they test something, we like to know about it.

"Bottom line on this Kamanchu thing, though, I'm afraid I can't help you much. On the other hand, I'd be derelict in my responsibility if I didn't ask why CSA is suddenly showing interest in Kamanchu again."

Baxter was understandably cautious. "Mind you,

this CSA stuff is still all new to me, Clark. In addition to which, I don't as yet understand everything I know about all of this. But . . . according to one of those young bucks at the meeting today, the CSA received a report from the Swiss Seismological Service in Zurich. That report indicates someone recently conducted an underground nuclear test in that area. In fact, it was just a couple of days ago—and that blast, according to Zurich, was set off just inside the Mongolian border. That, I'm afraid, is all I know about it."

Clark Barrows had never learned to focus his craggy smile. It wandered. "Well, if it was our Russian friends, they're in violation of the treaty. On the other hand, if it was the Chinese, they've been doing it all along. Of course, most of the time we know where and when—but this is one I haven't heard about yet. Notice that I added the word 'yet.' If the Chinese are at it again, I'll hear about it."

Baxter was almost apologetic. "Try to understand where I'm coming from, Clark. For the better part of the last twenty years I've been hearing about situations in a briefing room where I'm sent out to conduct my own investigation, draw conclusions, and report back. Now all of a sudden, I'm looking at satellite composites, computer-enhanced images, and a bunch of damned printouts."

Barrows laughed.

"Not to mention I'm in learning mode and not real comfortable with the fact I've got a bunch of junior officers and computer jockeys interpreting the situation for me. Know what I mean?"

Clark nodded. "Believe it or not, the same thing

that's happening to you now, happened to me a number of years back. Let's face it, the truth is, the years are starting to catch up with us old farts. These kids they're recruiting for us have a whole lot of tools at their disposal that you and I don't begin to understand, don't want to take the time to master, and don't completely trust. To make matters worse, these kids are convinced their tools are more reliable and more valuable than our experience or any advice we can give them. Know how I know?"

Baxter shook his head.

Barrows reached into his coat pocket, hauled out his vest secretary, and dug around until he located a small piece of paper. "Mary and I were having dinner at a little Chinese restaurant the other night and I found this in my fortune cookie. It says, 'Technology is your friend.' Now all I have to do is believe it and accept it. I mean, what the hell; if it's in a fortune cookie it has to be the truth. Doesn't it?"

Baxter laughed. "I suppose you're right, Clark. I guess if I can be trained to turn the controls of an F-16 over to a damn computerized pilot, I ought to be able to learn to trust a snot-nosed twenty-five-year-old with a computer and a handful of satellite photos."

Barrows continued to smile as he signaled the waiter for menus. "So much for Kamanchu. Now what else can I do to help you get situated?"

"We can go to priority two. You can tell me where I can find a decent apartment. Another week in the BOQ listening to rock music and I'll start talking to myself."

"Now you're getting into the hard part. Finding you suitable living accommodations in this town could be a whole lot tougher and take a great deal longer than bringing you up to speed on the situation at Kamanchu."

Marathon Key, Florida
1-5

Rick's Shanty was the watering hole of choice for most of the locals on Marathon Key. Rick Casey had worked hard at making it that way. Two blocks off and south of Highway 1, it was tucked away on a corner of the key where few tourists headed north or south would find it. It was a sanctuary for people with skin the color and texture of a good Tex Tan saddle and a minimalist sartorial attitude.

It was approaching mid-afternoon, with the Florida sun hammering down more like July than late October, when a red Chrysler Sebring convertible pulled into the cramped parking lot and turned a few heads. But by the time the driver had crawled out and stretched, and the locals had had an opportunity to appraise him, they had decided he looked like one of their own.

Thomas Jefferson Seacord—most people called him T. J.—was in his element. Oklahoman by birthright, Californian by education, and a nomad by choice, he was on his way north after spending three days with his daughter, Lucy, in Key West, and was eager for the opportunity to renew ties with old friends.

When he walked into the bar, a few heads turned, but the majority of Rick's denizens appeared to be preoccupied with the more serious chores of drinking and doing what they could to avoid the heat. It was hot in Marathon for the time of year.

By the time he had worked his way to the bar, he had been assessed, cataloged, and either accepted or written off by everyone in the room except the attractive thirty-something brunette behind the counter. "You look like a man in search of something cold to drink," she cooed. "What'll it be?"

"I'll start with the coldest Bud in your cooler," Seacord said, "and a question. Where's the owner?"

The woman's eyes brightened and she leaned forward with her elbows on the bar. "Let me guess, you're T. J.? Right? Damn, for once Rick was on target, you do look like Sean Connery. A tad more hair, maybe, and younger of course. Say something sexy so I can see if you sound like him too."

Seacord laughed. "I'll give you odds Sean Connery wouldn't take kindly to that. He makes a helluva lot more money than I do and he doesn't have to contend with an Oklahoma drawl."

It was the woman's turn to laugh. "Honey, I don't know whether anyone ever told you this or not, but when you look like him you don't need money. And just for the record, if I had known there was someone like you available, I wouldn't have married your friend, Rick."

"I take it you're Marlo. Rick told me about you."

"Not too much, I hope."

"Just enough to make you sound intriguing. Is the flight commander around?"

"Hell, yes, he's around. He's been looking forward to seeing you ever since you called and said you'd be stopping by. You're all he's talked about since he heard you were coming." She tilted her head to one side as she gave Seacord the once-over. "On the whole, though, I have to confess I'm a little disappointed. I'm surprised to see you aren't ten feet tall. To hear Rick tell it, you walk on water, eat nails for breakfast, and leap over tall buildings. But he didn't tell me the most important thing. You aren't married."

Seacord held up his left hand.

"I don't see any wedding ring. Hey, if I had known that, I'd have had some of my girlfriends lined up to entertain you."

Seacord was still grinning. "Unfortunately I won't be around long enough for that. I'm due back in Washington the day after tomorrow. My plane leaves Miami at noon tomorrow."

Two hours later, on a broad expanse of cypress decking sheltered by a sun-bleached awning that overlooked the water and a twenty-eight-foot Sea Sprite tied up behind the bar, Rick Casey and Thomas Jefferson Seacord were still trying to bring each other up to speed. Their conversation had meandered through the twenty or so years since the days when Casey had been T. J.'s flight instructor at Randolph, right up until the day Casey had resigned his commission and set out to fulfill a lifelong dream of becoming a sun-tanned nomad in the Florida Keys.

"You should have seen me, T. J. I drifted around for a couple of years, fished all day, played poker all night, chased women, spent most of my money, and then one night I met Marlo. I spent the better part of the next six weeks tryin' to figure how the hell a guy like me, on the cusp of the big six-zero, could propose to someone half my age. Then, one night while we were tippin' a few beers, she up and asked me to marry her. She said she felt compelled to make an honest man out of me. I reminded her I was damn near twice her age, but she said it didn't matter. So we got hitched.

"A year later we found this place on Marathon, hocked our souls, bought it, and settled down. Now we work like a couple of slaves all day, screw our brains out all night, and get up the next morning and start all over again."

Seacord finished his beer and stared out at the water. He was enjoying himself. "Well, it sure as hell looks like you found what you were looking for. Anytime you're so inclined, I'll trade you places."

Rick Casey shook his head. "No, thanks. I want no part of that three-ring circus I hear you're involved in up in Washington these days. I haven't had to salute anyone except my banker since I burned my uniforms. Speaking of uniforms, where's yours?"

"Haven't worn one in years. After they grounded me and informed me I would be spending the rest of my Air Force career behind a desk, I resigned. I went back to Oklahoma and started ranchin' again. Then one night I got a call from a fellow by the name of Clark Barrows. He said he wanted me to come to Washington, said he was sending me a plane ticket. Can't tell you why I went, but I did. Next thing I knew I was back in training again and working for something called G7.

"Two years ago I was on assignment and got caught in a little fracas down in Panama, took a slug just above the heart. I'm told I damn near bought my last piece of real estate. When I was whole again they put me on special assignment, which is another way of saying damn near retired. Then I got a call. This affair with Chen Ton is the first time I've been back in the saddle since then."

Rick Casey was shaking his head. "How old are you now?"

"Forty-five and thinkin' maybe I should give it up."

"Why not? The marina on the other side of the key is for sale. Why don't you buy it? Marlo and I would love to have you for a neighbor."

Seacord rejected his friend's invitation with an audible sigh. "As wonderful as it sounds, for the time being it's out of the question. If you read the newspapers at all, you know what's goin' on up north."

Rick Casey slumped back in his chair and studied T. J.'s face. "Well, I know you're involved in this Chen Ton matter. I been reading about it in *Newsweek*. What's the scoop?"

Even though they had known each other a long time, Casey was quick to get the impression his old friend was slightly reluctant to talk about the situation. At the same time, T. J. was aware that he was probably being overly reticent about something that seemed to be nightly fare on the front page of every newspaper and network news programs.

"There was a time," he said, "when three different people, all reasonably reliable sources, claimed they had some kind of proof Chen Ton was pullin' the strings on Ben Bridgewater prior to the Senator's murder. The problem is, two of those people are already dead. I'm the third."

Casey winced. "So, how the hell did you get involved?"

"The night after Bridgewater's body was found in that Washington hotel, Chen Ton flew to Macao. Why Macao? Seems obvious, doesn't it? Either way, I was a face Chen Ton wasn't familiar with, and they put me on a plane to follow him. We were reasonably certain that once he got to Macao he would disappear behind some very closed doors. And he probably would have if I hadn't been able to muscle him into a hotel room, get in touch with the U.S. consulate, and hold him there until we could get the necessary paperwork and approvals from the Portuguese to extradite him back to the ZI. By the time I got him back to the States, the other two so-called reliable sources were dead. All of a sudden it was my word against his. To complicate matters, the Chinese started waving the diplomatic-immunity flag."

"Diplomatic immunity? I thought he was a businessman."

"Actually, he's a little bit of both. Officially Chen holds the position of chargé d'affaires at the Chinese embassy in Washington. But he also owns an import/export firm operating out of Baltimore. That was the company laundering the money that was being passed along to Bridgewater. And if that doesn't impress you, the CIA also believes he is the number-one man in The Council."

"Do you think Chen Ton actually killed Bridgewater?"

Seacord shook his head. "No, but we're convinced he is the one who arranged to have the Senator killed."

Casey lapsed into a brief silence. "I guess I don't understand. On the other hand I don't have to. That's why they pay you the big bucks."

Seacord laughed.

"At any rate, I don't envy you, T. J. At this stage of my life the kind of fast track you're on doesn't hold much appeal. When the moon comes up I'd rather take a stroll along the water's edge or hunker down between the sheets with Marlo." There was another pause, slightly awkward. "I hear you and Kat split. When Marlo and I take a day trip to Miami, I usually pick up a copy of the *Post* and read her column. Every now and then I see her on one of those talk shows. She still looks good."

Seacord was quiet for several minutes. "The parting was amicable enough, I guess. She got custody of our daughter and a slice of my paycheck for child support. Two days after a Maringo County judge made it official, I got orders to ship to the South Pacific. We didn't see each other for two years. By that time I got back to the States she had a new life, a syndicated column, a radio talk show, and whatever rancor either of us might have been feeling when we left the courtroom that day had pretty much dissipated. Now at least, when we see each other, we're halfway civil."

"Do you see her often?"

"She pops up every now and then. She's operating out of Washington these days."

Rick finished his beer and set the bottle back on the table. "Marlo tells me you're cutting out early tomorrow morning. Anything I can do to change your mind?"

Seacord's face brightened. "Yeah, tell Marlo to dig

up one of those friends of hers she was telling me about earlier. I'll buy a couple of bottles of wine, and we'll take that Sea Sprite of yours out for a midnight sail. I can sleep on the flight back to Washington."

Hatmaanumbe
Solonge Valley
Northern Mongolia
1-6

Abjoe Chevaan sat on his porch watching and waiting. Behind him an oil lamp was doing little to penetrate the inky darkness. Abjoe Chevaan was used to the ritual of watching and waiting. In the spring he waited for the ewes to present him with a crop of lambs just as he waited for the pastures in the high country to turn a lush green. In the summer he waited again, this time for that same spring crop of lambs to quit suckling and gain strength. Then, as the warm days of summer passed, he waited for the days to shorten and the breezes to cool so that he could return home again.

Now, as Reanna busied herself putting the children down for the night, he watched, waiting for the moon to reappear from behind the clouds and draw the late October sky out of its somber mood.

There was much Abjoe needed to tell his wife. In many ways it had been a disappointing season. The spring lambs had not fared well, many of them had died, and even those that survived were sickly. To make matters worse, some of his prize ewes were showing signs of the same strange malady. On this day alone he had come upon the carcasses of no less than three of the creatures; bloated, stomachs distended to twice normal size, and evidence they had been bleeding from their nostrils and mouth prior to their to their death.

When Reanna finished her chores, she returned to the porch and sat down beside her husband. "I have something for you," he said, reaching into his pocket. "I found it in the rocks near the river where the flock drank."

Reanna's dark eyes appraised the tiny silver chain and she smiled. "It is lovely," she said. "But do you not agree that the river is a curious place to find such a gift."

Abjoe Chevaan put his arm around his wife's shoulder and hugged her gently. "I found it not long after the ground shook. That was the night of the terrible sounds. For a long time after the shaking quit I thought I could hear the sounds of the night creatures crying out in pain."

At that point Abjoe paused for several moments before he began again. "Would you think I was mad if I told you that after the ground shook I was certain I heard sounds like those of men dying?"

It was Reanna's turn to comfort her husband. "The sounds when the earth shakes do not trouble me so much. I am more concerned about our flock," she admitted. "With the loss of so many spring lambs, it will be difficult for us."

"It is not just the lambs," Abjoe sighed, "I counted no less than ten dead ewes in just the last three days. Even more troubling is the way they died. I have reasoned that it is perhaps the grasses in the high meadows. I have never grazed them as high before."

Again it was Reanna's logic about such matters that manifested itself. "But if the entire flock grazed the same meadows, would they not all be sick? When did you first notice that they were ill?"

Abjoe thought back and recounted the days. "It seems to have begun only a few days ago, when I started to bring the flock down to the valley of the Solonge to begin our journey home. Often I let them graze there for two days, but this year the grass was brown and there was little for them to eat. They drank their fill and I moved them on. The next morning I found several dead lambs. The flock and even the dogs were . . ." Abjoe's words were suddenly cut off by a deep and wracking cough that lasted several minutes. It was the second such spasm of coughing since he had returned.

This time, however, Reanna was alarmed both by the intensity of the coughing spell and its duration. She stood up, went into their small sod and log home, and returned moments later with her elixir of vinegar and honey. As usual, Abjoe protested. Reanna's remedy for everything was the small brown bottle in which she kept her odious nostrum.

"I will worry about the flock after I take care of you," she said. She produced a small wooden paddle, dipped it into the jar, instructed her husband to open his mouth, and prepared to swab his throat. "Stand here, close by the light of the lamp, so that I can see what I am doing," she said.

Abjoe complied and opened his mouth. When he did, Reanna peered in and immediately stepped back.

"No wonder you are coughing. Your throat is covered with open sores and boils."

Abjoe Chevaan dismissed his wife's concern with a wave of his hand, but the next morning he was dead.

Chapter Two

Kirensk Sibiriskove
2-1

Flight General Ivan Kisovovich finished reviewing the photographs, laid them upon his desk, leaned back in his chair, tented his sausage-sized fingers, and continued to listen as Dr. Chernov interrogated the young flight officer.

For the past thirty minutes the gist of the questions had been much the same. Each time Chernov managed to phrase them differently, but they were probing, repetitious, and always asked as though she suspected the young pilot of committing some kind of crime.

"I would remind the doctor that Lieutenant Slovin is not on trial here," Kisovovich interrupted. "He is here only because he wishes to cooperate and answer your questions."

Chernov was quick to defend her methodology. "Nor do I regard my repeated questions as an indictment or a test, General," she snapped. "I am simply trying to determine if there is anything he has overlooked. At the Institute we are taught that initial recall is often superficial in nature, and only through constant probing and examination of the most minute details in any given event are we likely to uncover critical information. To address your concerns, however, I would again ask the lieutenant if he objects to my line of questioning."

The young officer shook his head, glanced at his general, and offered a wry smile. "I am happy to have the opportunity to answer Dr. Chernov's questions," he said. "As the general has no doubt observed, she is much prettier than our squadron debriefing officer."

Kisovovich, who bordered on being a chain smoker, was amused by Slovin's response and lit another cigarette. By now the litany of questions, like the cloud of blue gray smoke that hung over the room, had become a blur and he found himself turning his thoughts to other matters. Had anyone thought to ask, Ivan Kisovovich would readily have admitted to a lengthy list of other concerns. All of which he considered more important than listening to the woman from the Health Ministry try to determine what Slovin and his observer had actually seen.

"Once again, Lieutenant, when did you first notice the defoliation?" Chernov asked.

"The flight observer pointed it out," Slovin repeated. "When I looked down I could see what he was talking about. The banks on both sides of the Solonge were brown. Usually this time of year the landscape is green because of the rains. The brown was of interest to us only because the river flows north into the Egiyn Gol and eventually into Ozero Baykal. If there was some sort of contamination or problem, we thought we should report it. That is why I mentioned it to my debriefing officer when I turned over the film."

Rebi Chernov picked up the photographs and began to systematically leaf through them again. "Is this the discoloration you are speaking about?" The photographs had been taken with a high-resolution camera and a special film developed for evaluating variations in ground cover. As she held them up, she pointed at an area that appeared to be a bright orange-red on the image.

"That is the area," Slovin confirmed. "As you can see, it is apparent for several kilometers."

"Dr. Chernov," Kisovovich interrupted. "May I ask what you intend to do with this information?" He was leaning forward in his chair now as though he had heard something that alarmed him.

Chernov's face reflected her surprise at the general's question. "I will report it, of course. The Health Ministry insists on being alerted to potential health hazards to our people. As you well know, General, Lake Bakyal is very popular. Even though the winter will soon be setting in, next summer thousands of our people will be visiting the area. We do not want them to walk unaware into a situation where their health will be compromised."

"Nyet," Kisovovich thundered. He was shaking his bulbous head. "You will make no such report."

Rebi Chernov, caught off guard by the general's sudden display of ire, studied his expression for several moments until she regained her composure. "I must insist on knowing why," she said. "I have orders to—"

Kisovovich cut her off. "Leave the room, Lieutenant," he grunted. "I would speak with Dr. Chernov alone." Slovin stood up, saluted, and left. The moment the door closed behind him, Kisovovich leaned forward again. He was still glowering, but he had regained much of the superficial composure Chernov had come to associate with the man. "I am telling you there will be no such report, Dr. Chernov, and I am telling you this for the simple reason that I will not permit it. Why? Because there is a matter of national security involved here.

"As you know, Kirensk is an aviation test facility, but it has another and, at times, an even more important purpose. From Kirensk we monitor the activity of our neighbors to the south, east, and west." Then he asked a question that surprised her. "Do you play chess, Dr. Chernov?"

The woman shook her head. "Not often," she admitted.

"Chess is quite unique. It is a game in which your opponent can see your every move and has time to study that move before he must respond. It is a chess game we play with the Chinese. We tell ourselves that they do not know we are watching them . . . just as they choose to believe we do not know they are observing what goes on here at Kirensk. Do you understand?"

Chernov's face was flushed. She did not respond.

"The important thing," Kisovovich continued, "is that this maintains a kind of disagreeable and annoying status quo. Which, for the time being, is exactly what both we Russians and the Chinese want—a status quo."

"But if you know each other's secrets, what is the—"

Kisovovich cut her off, but his manner had slowed to the point of being plodding. "A number of years ago, our Chinese friends began constructing a military installation just south of the Mongolian-Russian border. We were able to monitor the extent of their activity from our satellites as well as high-altitude aircraft. Our surveillance was justified. That facility, now known as Zijin Mountain, was built complete with a number of missile silos and a runway that would accommodate long-range bombers.

"Not long after, the Kamanchu area was hit by an earthquake. There was extensive damage. Then our Chinese comrades did a most curious thing; they dismantled the runway and appeared to downgrade the facility. But that first curiosity was followed by still another. They then built a railroad spur from Kamanchu that connected to the main line leading to Ulan Bator."

"I am afraid I do not understand," Chernov said. "Why would they—"

"Close the facility," Kisovovich finished for her,

"and build a railroad? Excellent question, and one that I would not have expected from someone at the Health Ministry. The answer, we now believe, is that the abandoned missile silos, all quite conventional and quite apparent from our satellite photos, were simply a ruse. The Chinese were clever. While we continued to take our pictures from above, they were busy constructing another set of launching devices underground, ones well hidden from our cameras."

Chernov listened intently.

"The question then becomes who or what are they preparing to attack, and when do they intend to launch that attack? Is it possible to build and conceal a missile launching system underground? The answer is a most emphatic yes. Our American friends have been doing it for years.

"Are we alarmed that Beijing readily admits that approximately twenty percent of the long-range nuclear missiles in the former Soviet arsenal are now in their hands? The answer, Doctor, is yes. However, knowing the frequent animosity and strained relations between our two countries, would you deny there is reason to believe that some of those missiles are now in Kamanchu and perhaps even aimed at us?"

Rebi Chernov, seldom at a loss for words, suddenly did not know what to say. What Kisovovich was describing was a convoluted international intrigue that she was not prepared to discuss. Officials at the Health Ministry in Moscow had said nothing about what the general was calling the real nature of the Kirensk outpost. Did they know? She had believed what she was told, that Kirensk was a testing facility, nothing more.

Could she condemn her superiors for deceit when it was possible they knew nothing about it? She continued to look at Kisovovich wondering how much he had not revealed. "But if the Chinese have found a way to conceal their efforts at this facility, how can you expect to learn anything by continuing to fly over this place you call Kamanchu?"

Kisovovich exhibited one of his rare smiles. "You do not think entirely like a humanitarian, Dr. Chernov, or you would not be so quick to ask such incisive questions. Yes, the Chinese know that we scrutinize their every movement at Kamanchu, but there is little they can do about it. They protest to their former comrades in the Mongolian government, but to no avail. While our friends in Ulan Bator remain a thinly guarded protectorate of the Chinese government, they are philosophically more aligned with the form of Communism once adhered to in our beloved Mother Russia."

"And what about you, General? What philosophy do you embrace?"

"My philosophy in such matters is irrelevant. I am a military man, Dr. Chernov. I follow orders. I leave matters of metaphysics, moral and natural philosophy, and politics to those who are trained for such thought. I have been ordered to monitor and report on activity at Kamanchu and the Zijin Mountain facility. And that, Dr. Chernov, is precisely what I do. And I do so because that is the way this chess game is played. But we cannot act—not without irrefutable proof. Otherwise we would divulge the exact boundaries of our knowledge."

"Does it not concern you that we have uncovered

a potential health hazard in a region so close by our border?" Chernov persisted.

Kisovovich began gathering his papers. At some point in their conversation he had lit another cigarette, but the woman had not noticed when. Now he studied its presence in his hand as though its existence was a surprise to him. "If you are asking if I will relent and permit you to file your report, the answer is still no. I do not believe it is necessary to remind you, Dr. Chernov, that there is still a Kremlin. The Defense Ministry has ways of seeing that our national security is not jeopardized by the filing of an ill-conceived report that is at best nothing more than mere speculation, suspicion, and theory."

"But . . ." Chernov started to protest.

"Suspicion and theory," Kisovovich repeated.

Chernov persisted. "But you cannot deny the evidence of defoliation along the banks of the Solonge River, General. The nature and the intensity of that discoloration alone is evidence of a very strong contamination—a contamination that may well eventually flow into Lake Baykal."

"Tell me, Dr. Chernov, do you have irrefutable proof that what you say is true?" Kisovovich pressed.

"I have photographs that show . . ."

Kisovovich shook his head. "On the contrary, Dr. Chernov, if you are banking on the aerial photographs to document your concerns, then you have no evidence." He reached across the desk and scooped up the photographs. "I have the photographs, and I must reaffirm that I see nothing that alarms me. Is that quite clear?"

Rebi Chernov did not answer him.

Closed Senate
Subcommittee Hearing
Washington
2-2

"Do you understand the nature of our gathering here today, Agent Seacord?"

"I do, Senator."

"Very well then, in that case I would like to introduce the other members of this subcommittee. I am Senator Branca, to your left is Senator Clemens, and to your right is Senator Allen. As you were informed when you were subpoenaed to appear before this committee, we are reviewing circumstances surrounding the untimely demise of our colleague, Senator Bridgewater of Idaho.

"At the same time we will be looking into the alleged involvement of one Mr. Chen Ton, the chargé d'affaires at the Chinese embassy here in Washington.

"Having dispensed with all that, Agent Seacord, suppose you tell us a little more about yourself. We have been told that you have a somewhat unusual situation; that while you are not currently on active duty, as it were, with G7, you are activated from time to time to assist in one of their investigations. Is that correct?"

"It's a matter of money, Senator. Retirement takes a bit more than I had anticipated. If I could get by without an occasional paycheck from the agency, I wouldn't be here."

"You appear to be quite young to have retired so early," Branca observed.

Seacord cleared his throat. "I'm not certain that you need any more than I've already told you, Senator Branca, other than to say I served as a pilot in the Air Force prior to my stint with G7."

"Very commendable, Agent Seacord." Allen was the first to speak other than Branca. He was short, intense, wore thick glasses, and had a drawl. "Suppose you tell us how you came to be involved in all of this?"

Seacord hesitated while he took a sip of water. "As I'm sure the Senator already knows, the CIA launched an investigation into the affairs of Senator Bridgewater some eighteen months ago. That investigation came about as the result of a program on CBS that questioned the degree of Senator Bridgewater's involvement with the man you spoke of earlier, Chen Ton. . . ."

Branca interrupted as he shuffled through a stack of papers. "Bear with me, Agent Seacord, but am I to understand that Kat Collier, a columnist with the *Washington Post,* who first reported the relationship between Senator Bridgewater and Mr. Chen Ton, is also your wife?"

"Former wife," Seacord corrected.

Branca corrected his notes and turned to Clemens for the next question. "Are we to also understand you were not involved with the Bridgewater investigation at the time the CBS program aired?" asked Clemens.

"That is correct, Senator. I was helping out on my father's ranch down in Oklahoma at the time. I don't watch television much and I'm not big on newspapers. Consequently I didn't know much about the whole affair. But I should probably add that I'm not certain there even was an agency investigation at that point."

"Proceed."

"As I was saying, the CIA investigation revealed that in addition to his duties with the embassy and his business in Baltimore, Chen Ton was also the head of a secret organization known as The Council. One of the objectives of The Council was to obtain information about CIA operations and sell that information to terrorist groups in Iraq, Iran, Libya, and several other Middle East countries.

"The CIA is convinced that for the past four years Chen Ton's organization has been making known the identities of CIA operatives in those areas, as well as a number of other places."

"I take it G7 is a branch of CIA? Is that correct?" Branca asked.

"Actually, Senator, they are two separate entities. Although there is a close relationship," Seacord admitted. "CBS refers to us as the police department of the CIA. That's probably an acceptable way of explaining it. We're joined at the top, that's all."

"Would you explain how the information obtained by Chen Ton's organization damaged agency operations, Agent Seacord?"

"The CIA network was rendered ineffective in those areas where the identity of the agent was revealed. In some cases agents were killed. In others they were imprisoned."

"These are serious charges. You have proof?"

"It depends on what you call proof, Senator."

"Would you explain to the committee just exactly

how Senator Bridgewater fit into all of this?" Branca continued.

"To begin with, the investigation began when the CIA uncovered the fact that Chen Ton's business was acting as a conduit for illegal funds to Senator Bridgewater's last two election campaigns. Chen Ton was eager to make certain Bridgewater stayed in office because of his close ties with both the CIA and his position on the Armed Services Committee. Whether or not the Senator was actually aware of Chen Ton's role with organizations our government considered to be subversive, is unknown.

"My involvement came about when the CIA investigation of the relationship between Senator Bridgewater and Chen Ton came under scrutiny, and our government began to learn more about his activities. That's when G7 was called in. Why? Because the agency was convinced that by that time Chen Ton had managed to get several of his own people into places where sensitive information about CIA activities was available."

"Like the names and assignments of CIA operatives?"

Again Seacord nodded. "Exactly. G7 was called in because it was feared Chen Ton's people would be able to recognize the identity of any CIA operative that had been involved in the investigation up to that point. Like I said, while the CIA is taking care of things on the outside, G7 is taking care of things on the inside. Other than that, Senator, I am not at liberty to discuss our activities."

Seacord watched as both Clemens and Allen continued to take notes and Branca continued his questioning. "Tell me about Senator Bridgewater's death. Why do you think it was Chen Ton who arranged to have him killed?"

"The best theory advanced so far," Seacord began, "comes from our Deputy Director of Operations, Clark Barrows. He believes that when the story broke on CBS and with the follow-up articles in the *Post,* Senator Bridgewater decided to make a clean breast of things and admit his campaign had accepted sizeable amounts of money from Chen Ton. We also believe he intended to reveal he had helped Chen Ton get some of his people employed in some relatively sensitive government positions—primarily with investigative agencies."

"Go on."

"Our theory is that after CBS broke the story, there was a subsequent confrontation between Bridgewater and Chen Ton during which Bridgewater revealed his intentions to make known their relationship."

"If that had happened, Agent Seacord," Senator Clemens concluded, "assuming diplomatic immunity did not dictate otherwise, Mr. Chen Ton would have been out of business and probably put behind bars for a very long time. Is that the way you read it?"

"I do."

Branca was still nodding in agreement when he turned his attention back to Seacord. "Would you care to tell us where you were the night Senator Bridgewater died?"

"Three rows behind Chen Ton at a Knicks-Celtics exhibition game. His entourage included three other people, all reputable Chinese businessmen visiting this country as part of a trade mission. Their names are in the record. As Chen Ton has repeatedly pointed out, he has the perfect alibi."

"But the G7 DDO is convinced Chen Ton arranged the Senator's death. Correct?" Clemens asked, trying to clarify.

" 'Arranged' is probably the right word, Senator. It was made to look like a mugging gone wrong."

"Tell us about the flight to Macao," Branca pushed.

Seacord took another sip of water before he answered. "A series of articles in the *Washington Post* followed the CBS program. Between the articles and the program, they were beginning to unravel the relationship between Senator Bridgewater and Chen Ton. When that happened, the DDO figured Chen might use some ruse to try to leave the country. When he did, we were tipped off by an airline employee who recognized him when he purchased the tickets. He was buying his ticket under an assumed name and using a bogus passport. The ticket agent recognized him from the *60 Minutes* broadcast. They sold him a ticket, but managed to get me on the same flight. I phoned ahead when our flight landed in San Francisco. I requested and got all the cooperation I needed from the Macao police. We took him in when we landed in Macao. As a result I spent the next two days with Chen Ton locked up in a hotel room until we could get the necessary extradition papers. There was a member of the Macao police department outside the hotel room the entire time."

"At any time during that period did Chen Ton reveal anything that would tie him to the death of Senator Bridgewater? Or did he say anything that might incriminate him in conspiracy charges?"

"He did," Seacord said. "But he was equally quick to point out that there were no witnesses to our conversations, nor had the Attorney General been able to produce any witnesses to Senator Bridgewater's death."

"The man sounds rather confident, Agent Seacord. If he were to be implicated and tried in this matter, do you believe he is convinced that the issue of his involvement boils down to his word against yours?"

Seacord hesitated. "The last thing Chen Ton said to me when we landed in Washington was that this time G7 was in over its head. He said he could guarantee I would be dead long before he went to trial, and that if it happened sooner than later, it would look like an accident. Then he added—in all likelihood as an afterthought—that getting rid of me probably wouldn't be necessary because he was confident he would never be charged. I remember him laughing and telling me even if he was charged, the matter would never come to trial."

Branca wasn't finished. "Did Mr. Chen say why he thought he would not be tried?"

"He did, Senator. He said he had too many friends in too many of the right places."

"And what do you think, Agent Seacord?"

"I think he is underestimating us, Senator."

At that point Branca turned to the other two Senators and inquired if they had any further questions. When they indicated they had none, he turned back to Seacord. "I believe that is quite enough for today, Agent Seacord. My esteemed colleagues and I wish to thank you for your cooperation. Be aware, however, that there is always the chance we will have more questions as our investigation continues. If such an event occurs, we would require your further cooperation. Is that clear?"

Seacord nodded.

Ministry of Health
Slovadoka Pokavast
Moscow
2-3

For seventy-one-year-old Josef Chenko the day had been long, far too long. A wet, clinging snow had prevented him from taking his cherished noontime stroll through Komsomol Square. And what should have been no more than an hour-long meeting with the Jewish Council had taken the better part of the afternoon.

At an age when most of his contemporaries had retired, and with Chenko himself admitting to questionable health, he was quick to concede that he now found it difficult to do anything for three hours straight except sleep. The meeting with Ribowitz had required that he both forfeit his nap and pay attention to the old man's litany of complaints about the deplorable conditions in the Siborsk district.

Now, with only a thirty-minute meeting scheduled with Rebi Chernov, he could soon wrap up his day. The meeting with Chernov, he had decided when he scheduled it, would very probably be the highlight of his day.

Josef Chenko regarded Rebi Chernov as one of his rewards for still working when most men his age sought refuge in fine books, warm fires, and good vodka. So much did he look forward to seeing his young protégé that he found himself repeatedly returning to the window, staring out, and waiting for her car to pull into the parking lot. When he finally saw the black Zhiguli sedan wheel into the parking slot adjacent to his aging Pobedas, he knew she had arrived.

For Josef Chenko there was a definite advantage to wrapping up the day with Rebi Chernov. She was certainly the most attractive of his regional health advisors. And she was one of the few who did not grumble about underfunding, outdated computers, and their other misfortunes following the breakup of the old system. At age thirty-two, Rebi Chernov did not mince words, and she was one of his most competent inspectors. She was more than capable of conducting an off-site assessment of a remote military post and authoring a detailed report that reflected the true nature of the situation she had inspected. Chenko wished he could say as much for all the members of his staff.

Now, just moments before her arrival, he was again glancing down at his protégée's latest report detailing her inspection of the facility at Kirensk. It resonated with the same thoroughness and insight he had come to expect in all her memorandums. But, at the same time, Chenko had noticed a difference; Chernov had somehow hedged her report. When he'd questioned her about it, she had requested a one-on-one meeting with him stressing the word *yehnhehue*. Alone. He had agreed to the private meeting, but had been dismayed by the fact that the only time they could meet was late in the day when he was not at his best.

Now, at thirty-seven minutes after four o'clock, he heard her coming down the hall. The closer the time came for their meeting, the more Chenko realized how much he was looking forward to seeing her.

Rebi Chernov, in another day and given a different disposition, might well have been a model. She was slender, tall, graceful, and charming to distraction. Plus, she had the capacity for hard work, exhibited an uncommon interest in her duties, and possessed the endurance of a true problem-solver. She was, as one Ministry official had called her, "a jewel among cut glass."

Rebi Chernov was the only daughter of a Russian military officer and a woman who taught philosophy at Moscow University. From an early age she had been encouraged to study medicine. Chenko still recalled her answer when in her initial interview he had inquired whether or not she was or had ever been a Communist.

"I am whatever is necessary to obtain this position," she had replied. He was convinced she had been serious.

Now, as she stepped into his office, Josef Chenko was certain the atmosphere in his dour office would brighten. "It is good to see you," he said, standing up. "After a day of grappling with problems for which I no longer can summon a passion, you are my reward. How was your trip to Kirensk?"

Rebi smiled and sat down across the desk from him. She was wearing the obdurate uniform of the Health Ministry. Even so, Chenko thought she looked stunning. She crossed her legs and pointed to the file folder on Chenko's desk. "You tell me," she teased.

"Is it complete? Does it address your concerns?"

Chenko tapped his bony finger on the folder and assured her that it was no less than he had expected. "However, I must confess that I detected an undercurrent throughout your report. It reads as though there was something you wished to include but thought better of. Am I being a foolish old man reading things into reports that aren't there? Or is that why I am being rewarded with your presence so soon after your return?"

"How long have we known each other, Josef?"

Chenko thought back. "How long have you been with the Ministry, seven, eight years now?"

"Going on nine—and because I have learned there are few things worse than omitting important details in an inspection report, I felt it necessary to talk to you."

"Then I was right, there is something hidden between the lines."

"There is," she confirmed.

"Then what you wish to tell me should be held in confidence?"

"That is for you to decide. For my part, I have decided it should not be part of my report unless you determine that it should be included."

The old man looked hurriedly around his office, and managed a small, slightly lopsided smile. The gesture exposed a row of even yellow-white teeth, obviously not his own. "I see no KGB or GRU lurking in the shadows. Therefore I would assume it is safe for us to proceed."

Rebi Chernov opened her briefcase and laid three photographs on the desk. "What you are looking at is a series of digitally enhanced ground surveillance photographs taken from an altitude of nine thousand feet by one of our Mil Mi-8 helicopters. The photographs were taken at dusk with infrared K-t film." She paused before she confessed, "These are not the originals; they are copies. General Kisovovich does not know I have these. Perhaps I should also add he was most adamant about keeping the originals, denying me copies, and insisting that I omit this matter from my report."

"How did you obtain these?"

Rebi Chernov smiled. "Being a woman is not always a disadvantage. A young officer was gracious enough to make them for me."

Josef Chenko picked up his trusty magnifying glass. "Suppose you tell this old man what he is looking at?"

"These are photographs taken at various points along the Solonge River, east of the confluence of the Etano in an area some thirty kilometers south of the Mongolian-Russian border. Note the brown and red area along both banks of the river, and then notice that the discoloration extends from the location of Jingsan Bridge all the way to the confluence of the Egiyn Gol. Further know that when water is released from the Jingsan Dam south and east of there, it eventually forces the flow into Ozero Baykal."

"And this is cause for alarm?" Chenko questioned.

"The brownish area is an indication of extensive damage caused by some kind of pollution. The red area indicates damage of an even more severe nature. Also note that it is quite extensive."

Chenko continued to pore over the photographs for

several more minutes. "And what are these?" he questioned. He was pointing at a series of black spots spaced at random intervals along the shoreline.

"I have had some of the pictures magnified. What you see are the carcasses of dead animals, most of which are sheep, probably belonging to Mongol shepherds in the area. They dot the shoreline as far as the brown area extends."

"You know the cause of this—this pollution?"

Rebi Chernov was shaking her head before Chenko had the opportunity to finish his question. "At this point we know very little, certainly neither the cause nor the source. It begins somewhat north of what General Kisovovich informs me is an abandoned PRK facility that his flights continue to monitor on a routine basis."

"You advised General Kisovovich of your findings and mentioned your concerns?"

Rebi Chernov braced herself. This was the test. What would Chenko do with the information when she informed him that General Kisovovich insisted that her concerns about pollution and its source not be included in her report? She repeated the general's warning, then waited.

It was several moments before Chenko gave any indication that he had even heard what she said. "Old ways die hard." He finally sighed. "In the minds of many of our citizens, the State still comes before the welfare of the people. I knew Ivan Kisovovich when he was just a passionate young officer in the KGB. It may surprise you to know that we roomed together for a while at the Moscow City Collegium of Advocates."

"You were a member of the Party?" Rebi seemed surprised by her mentor's revelation.

"Look at me, my child. Look at me with inquiring eyes and without youthful respect for my title. Do you not see that I am old and often unfit to hold my position? How do you think I became the director of the Health Ministry?"

"I-I just-just never thought about . . ."

Josef Chenko tried to laugh. To his young colleague it sounded more like a wheeze. Still, it was the first time he had heard the usually articulate Chernov stammer. He dismissed the comment and continued. "And what exactly do you expect me to do with this information?" he asked.

"That is up to you. I have fulfilled my obligation; I have reported the condition." Her reply was surprisingly puritanical and uncompromising. It caught him off guard.

Again he waited several moments before reacting. Finally he labored up out of his chair and walked to the window again. He stood watching the unpleasant soup of snow and rain in the parking lot and the traffic on Gudonski just beyond. "Do not think that I did not hear everything you are telling me. On one hand, it would not sit well with his comrades in the Kremlin if I authorized you to press on with your investigation and advised you to ignore General Kisovovich's warnings. There could even be consequences for both of us if I did." Chenko turned his back to the window, propped his back against the sill, and looked at the woman. He folded his hands behind his back. "On the other hand, we would not be doing our job if we did not question the source of the contamination, would we?"

"Then you will permit me to include the matter in my report?"

Chenko held up his hand as if to fend off the question. "Give me a day or two to make some phone calls. Like our esteemed comrade General Kisovovich, I too am not without friends."

Gage Woods Condominiums
Belle Haven, Virginia
2-4

Thomas Jefferson Seacord spent most of his late-afternoon drive back to his apartment in a reflective state of mind. First there was the barrage of questions from the subcommittee to rethink. He could recall none that he would have answered differently. Then his thoughts turned to his old flight instructor, Rick Casey, and finally to the realization that his refrigerator had absolutely nothing in it. What was it his daughter said in situations like this? "Bummer." An empty apartment and an empty refrigerator—not exactly enticing.

When he shared his previous Washington apartment with his old roommate, Sham Chapman, he always knew there would at least be a cold six-pack in the fridge. But that had been yesterday or last year—Seacord figured time didn't matter when something was over. With Sham now sharing his digs with his new live-in girlfriend, Seacord was the odd man out.

Nevertheless, to Seacord's way of thinking, his new place in Gage Woods Condominiums had several things going for it. It was close to a supermarket, afforded him a halfway respectable view of the Potomac, was an easy drive to the office, and even more importantly, the complex's superintendent took care of things when he was out of town. Still, most of his worldly possessions remained tucked away in boxes for the simple reason he hadn't been in town long enough to unpack.

So far Seacord had met three of his neighbors. Number one was a young paralegal by the name of Marci Lincoln who looked good in a bikini—at least the one she'd been sunning herself in the day he moved in. Two and three were the young couple from Columbus, Ohio, who had introduced themselves that same day, presented him with a welcoming bottle of scotch, and promptly disappeared. He hadn't seen them since. There was a fourth unit, Marci had informed him, which was occupied by a pilot with United Airlines, but to date, Seacord and the pilot hadn't crossed paths.

By the time he pulled under the parking canopy, it had started to rain. He gathered up his papers, dashed across the parking lot into the foyer, checked his mail, climbed the stairs, and got a surprise. His door was open, Marci Lincoln was standing in the middle of the room, and his living room had been trashed. What little furniture there was in the room had been reduced to rubble.

"You, sir, are a terrible housekeeper," Marci said when she saw him.

"What the hell happened?" Seacord asked.

Marci shrugged her shoulders and made a sweeping gesture with her hand. "I came home, saw your door was open, peeked in, and this is what I found. Apparently someone doesn't care for the way you decorated. Seems like a rather shabby way of telling you, though."

Seacord appraised the damage, slowly working his way through the clutter. Walking into the bedroom, he looked around, then set his briefcase down. "Welcome to Gage Woods, huh?"

From there he walked to the second bedroom and found more of the same. Finally he started for the phone. "Guess I better report this, huh?"

Marci got to the phone ahead of him. "Let me do it. I would have already reported it I had thought you wouldn't mind someone poking around in your affairs. I mean, what with your picture being on television and all—you know, you being involved in that matter with that dead Senator."

Seacord would later recall that he was laughing as he watched her pick up the phone. That was when the room exploded. He remembered hearing Marci Lincoln's scream, remembered the acrid smell of explosives . . . and then his own circuitry shut down and his world went black.

"You're a very lucky man, Mr. Seacord," a little man was saying. "In fact, I'd almost go so far as to say you live a charmed life. Since they brought you in I've dug enough chunks of metal out of your hide to qualify for a salvage operator's license. Beats me how you avoided getting peppered in the eyes with this shrapnel. I removed seven of these ugly little pieces out of your face alone." He shoved a small stainless-steel emesis basin in front of Seacord's face and rattled the pieces around to demonstrate his collection.

Even though Seacord's vision was still somewhat blurred, he was able to make out the filmy image of a short, nervous, overweight little man with glasses. He was wearing green scrubs and tiptoeing around the examining table, squinting, peeling back Seacord's eyelids, poking him with his finger, and flashing his annoying little light into every hole he could find.

"Yes, sir," the man repeated. "Damned lucky." Finally he stepped away from the table, peeled off his latex gloves, and began putting away his instruments. "Bottom line, you don't look so good and you probably don't feel so good, but you're outta here just the same."

"What about Ms. Lincoln?" Seacord asked. "How is she?"

The fidgety little man with the thick glasses shrugged and informed him that, if he was referring to the woman who had been brought in with him, she had been taken to surgery. "At the moment that's all I can tell you." He started for the door, then paused. "Oh, I nearly forgot; stop at the desk on your way out. I'll leave a prescription for something that'll knock down some of the pain. I figure you'll probably need it before this night is over."

Seacord watched the door close, and got down off the examination table. He labored through the process of getting dressed in a shirt and trousers decorated with burn holes and bloodstains, then walked out into a dimly lit hospital corridor filled with the pungent odor of antiseptic. He heard the voices before he saw their owners. Gradually they emerged from the shadows.

"From the looks of you, you must be Seacord. Right?" one of the men asked. His voice was husky, like a bear with a cold, and there was the strong odor of coffee and cigarette smoke.

T. J. nodded. "Unfortunately."

"My name is Pesky and my partner over there is Detective Amos Washington. We're with the Virginia Bomb Squad. We'd like to ask you a few questions. Feel up to it?"

Seacord was still unsteady, but he managed a nod and began looking for a place to sit down. When he did, Pesky pulled a chair up next to him, unbuttoned his suit coat, loosened his tie, and sat down. His eyes were bloodshot and he looked tired. His partner, Washington, hung back, content to prop his back against the wall and remain standing.

"Any word yet on Marci Lincoln?" Seacord managed.

"Doctor Martin didn't tell you?"

Seacord shook his head.

Pesky lit a cigarette and looked at his partner. His voice was full of holes. "I'm afraid Ms. Lincoln didn't make it. She was dead when they brought her in."

Seacord felt his throat constrict, and for a moment he had difficulty breathing. There was an instantaneous dull ache behind his eyes, the kind men get when they wish they could cry. He looked at Pesky, then Washington; in the space of a few minutes they had managed to become part of his nightmare. He tried to stand up, but his knees refused to cooperate, and he slumped back down in the chair with his eyes closed.

Pesky waited for several moments before he muttered, "Sorry." He sounded sincere.

"Want to tell us what happened?" Washington pressed. Unlike Pesky, Washington didn't sound sincere; he just sounded tired.

Seacord was aware that his voice was cracking. "There isn't that much to tell, Detective. I got home around six-thirty. The door was open, Ms. Lincoln was there, and she offered to call the police to report that my apartment had been ransacked. She picked up the receiver, and you can figure out the rest."

Pesky dropped his cigarette on the floor, snuffed it out with his heel, and lit another. "Pipe bomb," he said, "loaded with shrapnel. Whoever did it knew what they were doing. They probably figured you'd come home, see everything torn up, and go for the phone. They'd be a long way away from the scene when you picked up that receiver."

"Incidentally, we know who you are," Washington said. "I recognized the name when we got the call from the local authorities. There ain't too many people around with a name like Thomas Jefferson something. I assume you know the question I have to ask. Do you think this could be tied to the Bridgewater-Chen Ton affair?"

Seacord was studying the designs in the tile floor. "I haven't had a helluva lot of time to do any thinking between then and now," he admitted. "Marci reached for the telephone and it was all over." Then he added, "But I'd give you short odds that it is."

"Well, we won't know much until we've had a chance to comb through the debris," Washington drawled. "But whoever did it sure as hell knew something about human behavior. Reaching for that telephone is the first thing nine out of ten people would do."

"In the meantime," Pesky cut in, "you won't be able to use your apartment—not until we've had a chance to go over it. Have you got a place to stay and a number where we can get in touch with you?"

Seacord wanted to tell them his thinking was still a little muddy. Finally he said, "I think so."

Pesky watched Seacord struggle to get out of his chair, and he said, "Why don't you let us make that call for you."

Ministry of Health
Moscow
2-5

Rebi Chernov was surprised at how quickly Josef Chenko got back to her. Only two days had passed since she had made her initial report to the Ministry's director when Chenko requested her presence at a meeting in his office on the next afternoon.

Now, at the end of a rainy but productive day, after hurrying through dinner with a friend at the Praga on Arbat Street, she found herself waiting outside her mentor's office. In typical fashion, she had used the day to her advantage. She had spent hours monitoring reports from Beijing, pored through back issues of the *Chin Ho Singh,* and even gone so far as to have one of the clerks in her section contact a relative in Ulan Bator. On balance she had learned very little of value, but there were three pieces of information that intrigued her.

One, Mongolian officials were aware that despite repeated PRK denials, there was still a good deal of activity at Kamanchu.

Two, on at least three separate occasions, a train carrying nuclear waste materials had passed through Ulan Bator bound for an undisclosed dumping site in the Gobi Desert. Furthermore, the article in the *Chin Ho Singh* speculated that the source of the waste was a top-secret military installation near Hatgal.

Three, there was an article published in an underground newspaper by a well-known former Party dissident. In it, he discussed the unauthorized sale of both technology and components for an RBMK pressurized water nuclear reactor to the Chinese. Rebi had attempted to verify the latter, but her contacts at the Kremlin steadfastly denied that such a sale to anyone outside of the country had been made.

Armed with these bits of knowledge, she was prepared to argue with Chenko if he decided to turn his back on the situation.

When Chenko finally opened the door for her and invited her into his office, she was surprised. There was another person present: a man, tall, slender, white-haired, and attired in a three-piece suit. Like Chenko, he was smiling. He stood up when she entered the room.

"Dr. Chernov," Chenko said, "I would like you to meet an old colleague, Dr. Miles Hamilton. Miles is a very dear friend of mine."

Before Rebi Chernov could acknowledge her mentor's introduction, Hamilton was telling her how delighted he was to meet her. "Josef has been telling me what a find you were for his department," Hamilton began. His Russian, unlike some of Chenko's other Western friends, was impeccable. Rebi couldn't decide whether he sounded more like an Englishman or if she had finally met an American who didn't slur his words.

Despite Hamilton's charm, Rebi was unable to mask her dismay at finding someone else in Chenko's office. She had counted on her meeting with the aging director being an opportunity to further discuss the situation south of Kirensk. "You will forgive me, Dr. Hamilton, if I appear ungracious, but I was under the impression that—"

Chenko cut her off. "And that is exactly why Miles is here, to discuss the situation that has been distressing you. We are fortunate. Dr. Hamilton is able to join us because he is attending a symposium here in Moscow. I invited him here for the express purpose of examining your photographs so we could learn more about the matter." When Chenko finished, he paused long enough to move around his desk and take a seat. "Dr. Hamilton is with the International Health Organization. His area of concern just happens to be in the very arena that you have brought to my attention."

Hamilton settled back in his chair and crossed his legs. "Josef tells me you have some rather interesting photographs. May I see them?"

Rebi Chernov's expression revealed her relief. She glanced quickly at Chenko for approval, removed the photographs from her briefcase, and handed them to the American. "As I explained to Dr. Chenko when I returned from a recent inspection trip, these photographs were taken from a Mil Mi-8 aircraft at an altitude of nine thousand feet with infrared K-t film. Note the evidence of extensive pollution along the banks of the river."

Hamilton spent several minutes studying the images, and finally laid them on Chenko's desk. "You should applaud your young colleague, Josef; she has uncovered something that might easily be overlooked in a routine assessment of the situation. . . ."

Before he had finished complimenting her, Rebi had handed him a map of the area, pinpointed the precise location on the Solonge, and traced the flow where that river eventually emptied into the Etano. "Admittedly, it is a remote area," she said. "But if the source of this pollution continues unabated, I believe it would eventually pose a health hazard to the Ozero Baykal."

Hamilton was frowning. "Have you contacted the authorities in Ulan Bator about this matter?"

"I was awaiting Dr. Chenko's permission to go forward with this information."

"My colleague tells me that there are also political ramifications related to this. Is that correct?"

"It is a game we Russians and Chinese choose to play." Chenko sighed. "A number of years ago, the Chinese initiated a great deal of activity in that area. According to our sources, it was believed they were constructing a military installation of some kind. Then there was an earthquake causing considerable damage—what was done, was apparently undone. After that, it was thought our Chinese friends dismantled the facility. Despite that fact, there was a continued, albeit a seemingly modest, level of activity. Rebi and

I have recently learned that our planes in Kirensk continue to monitor the situation."

Hamilton's frown deteriorated into a scowl. "Are you suggesting that whatever activity the Chinese are currently conducting may have been the source of this pollution?"

"Did *I* imply that?" Chenko smiled.

Hamilton shifted in his chair. "Josef, we are old friends, but I'm not certain I understand what you expect me to do with this information."

Chenko leaned forward with his arms on the desk. His palsied hands were shaking. "The situation of Dr. Chernov and myself can best be described as delicate, my friend. If we bring this matter to the attention of certain high officials in our government, they will be confronted by General Kisovovich and his comrades in the Kremlin. The matter will die there and we will have done nothing to determine the cause of this pollution or alleviate Dr. Chernov's concerns. If, on the other hand, you were to indicate your distress concerning this situation to your colleagues back in America, it could perhaps elevate this matter to the point where a thorough investigation would be demanded."

"You are thinking maybe the United Nations?" Hamilton questioned.

"Perhaps."

Hamilton laughed. "You are a devious old rascal, Josef. IHO raises the flag, shows our concern, gets the ball rolling, the UN steps in, and you and Dr. Chernov are above suspicion, correct?"

Chenko was pleased. "It will appear that you are merely expressing concern about data you have obtained from your own satellites, will it not?"

Hamilton looked at Rebi. "I'm flying back to Washington tomorrow, Dr. Chernov. I think I know where to start to get the ball rolling. Be aware, though, like so many things in my country, it may take us a while to get in gear. I'm certain you can appreciate that there is a great deal of red tape in a situation like this. But I can guarantee you this much: We will eventually get back to you either with some answers or a plan. Is that satisfactory?"

Rebi was delighted. She looked fondly at the man who had become a combination of confidant and advisor as well as her immediate supervisor. "You were right, Josef," she said. "You do have friends in the right places."

Chapter Three

1910 High Terrace
Ravenwood, Virginia
3-1

Mary Barrows repeatedly referred to it as both a grieving and healing process. Regardless of what it was called, Seacord had learned to hate it. He had spent the previous six days indulging feelings of guilt and remorse while nature supposedly was working her painfully slow curative process. He was tired of reading, tired of watching television, tired of being confined, and tired of constantly being admonished not to do this or that.

Throughout the ordeal, the Barrowses had been wonderful. Clark had picked him up at the hospital the night of the explosion, driven him to their home in Ravenwood, and done, within reason, everything he could to make his friend comfortable. When Clark wasn't around, Mary took over. It was Mary who saw to it that T. J. got to the doctor, Mary who drove him to the cemetery the day they buried Marci Lincoln, Mary who cooked his meals and made certain he was eating right. And it was Mary who fended off calls from T. J.'s friends, coworkers, and reporters.

For Seacord the most difficult part of the ordeal had been when he'd come face-to-face with Marci Lincoln's family. The Lincolns appeared to be good people—honest, hardworking, and as he learned, devoted to their daughter. They even talked about how they had pleaded with her not to move to a big city like Washington. Through it all, Seacord was convinced his expressions of regret and bereavement had been inadequate. Reflecting back, he realized it was one of the few times in his life when he wished he could have been more articulate. On three different occasions after the Lincolns had gathered their daughter's belongings, packed them into a U-Haul trailer, and headed home, he had tried to pen a letter to the couple. But the words never seemed to come out the way he wanted them to, and he finally gave up.

It was left to his former wife, Kat, to level the playing field. At Mary's urging she had stopped by two days after the bomb went off, and it was obvious she had not been prepared for what she saw when she walked into the room. His face was still swollen, and the montage of fresh scars and bandages caught her off balance. Her stay lasted no more than twenty or thirty minutes before she dashed off professing to be already late for an editorial meeting. Seacord doubted that, but she was, after all, still Kat . . . and there wasn't that much to say anyway.

Now, however, four days after her initial visit, and with the Barrowses attending a charity event somewhere in the city, Seacord was driving for the first time, and pulling into the parking lot of the Green Frog to have dinner with his ex-wife. He was both looking forward to and dreading the occasion at the same time. True, it would be a pleasant change from the intentionally bland but healing diet Mary Barrows had been serving up. On the other hand, he had to admit he never knew which Kat was going to actually show up at their infrequent meetings.

The former Kat Seacord—better known to the millions of readers of her syndicated column as Kat Collins—could be counted on to be unpredictable. Like her signature, scrawled under her picture in the column, which always amused Seacord. Kat liked to tell people her handwriting was a rebellion against the nuns that had tried to teach her penmanship, but the truth was, her handwriting had been terrible since the second grade.

The Green Frog was an out-and-out tavern, famous for its seafood and its piano player. It had long been Seacord's favorite haunt when he was trapped in Washington. Kat knew that, and he surmised that was the reason she'd chosen it. For her, the Green Frog amounted to a monumental concession. She would have preferred something with a little more glitz, where she knew the chef by name, and with a room where she could make one of her patented grand entrances. Still, when T. J. selected a table not far from the piano bar, it was his preference, and not necessarily Kat's. He ordered the usual, a Black and White and water, then settled back to nurse his drink and listen to the Frog's current piano player—an attractive young woman in a skintight white evening dress.

Seacord figured he had plenty of time to enjoy the music; when one made a date with Kat, one usually waited.

Kat Collins, now in her early forties, was still an auburn-haired stunner. When she entered a room, people took notice. When she departed, the room seemed just a little bit empty. She had emerald green eyes, a mesmerizing smile, and a biting wit. She could alternate between sarcastic, caustic, sweet, or vulnerable, all within a heartbeat.

Now, less than five minutes late, she was standing in front of him, and it was obvious that more than a few people in the room recognized her. "Hi, flyboy," she cooed. "How about buying a girl a drink?"

Her jeans and sweatshirt took him by surprise. Kat had dressed down for the occasion, but despite her efforts to grunge it up, she still looked great.

"What's your pleasure?" he asked.

"Dry martini, or have you forgotten?"

Seacord signaled the bartender, and again wondered first why he had agreed to meet her, then why he would have ever considered otherwise. The minute she'd walked into the room he'd been reminded of the fact that some things would never change, like the fact that even after all these years, this woman could still play with his mind.

"I'm glad you called," he finally admitted. "I've been rapidly developing a first-class case of cabin fever. Mary, bless her heart, watches me like a hawk. The minute she sees me walk into or out of the room, she promptly warns me I might be overdoing it."

Kat smiled. It wasn't a real smile, but more like one of her publicity stills. She waited while the server placed her martini on the table in front of her. Then she pursed her lips. "Look, Thomas. Let's forgo the small talk and cut to the real reason why I'm here. First, I don't like getting the runaround. Second, I intend to do something about it. Why the hell is everyone being so vague? I can't get a straight answer out of Clark, and Mary isn't much better. Even Chet David acts like he doesn't know what the hell I'm talking about when I ask about you."

Seacord shrugged. "Maybe they think I need protecting."

"Is that all that you can do? Shrug? You know I don't like that cowboy non-verbal shit. I deserve better than that."

Seacord shrugged again.

Kat lowered her voice. "Consider the fact that I've been to see you and talked to you on the phone twice. Each time, you sounded like you're in a damn fog. What's going on? That's not the Thomas I know."

Seacord took a sip of scotch, and felt the pleasant warmth burn its way down his throat. "Okay, what do you need to know?"

"Well, you can start by telling me just how bad

you're hurt? Clark is always vague as hell when he returns my calls. Mary doesn't say much more."

"Hey, what can I tell you? It was a pipe bomb. You know that. Pipe bombs tend to do nasty things to people—you know that as well. Added to that is the fact that if it hadn't been for me, that Lincoln girl might still be alive. She deserved better."

"Nevermind Marci Lincoln. It was you they were trying to kill," Kat reminded him. "And from the looks of you, they damn near succeeded. Your face still looks like hell."

Seacord continued to shrug. He didn't like the way the conversation was going. "She was a nice kid. Her only problem was she was in the wrong place at the wrong time."

Kat leaned forward, frowning. "When I invited you here, I thought maybe we'd have a couple of drinks, make some small talk—you know, the civilized little elements of social grace you never mastered—and then I would tell you what *I* learned."

Seacord braced himself. "What do you mean, 'learned'?"

She ignored his question, answering with one of her own. "Mary tells me you're developing into a real masochist over this whole affair. She says you're beating yourself up over that girl. Is that true?" When Kat wanted to or had to, she could get straight to the point. "What was your involvement with her? Were you sleeping together?"

"Do I ask you about your private life?"

Kat shook her head. "I ask only because I'm not certain how to word what I have to tell you."

"For the record, I wasn't sleeping with her—but

who knows what would have developed? The Marci Lincoln I knew was bright, young, well educated, extremely attractive, and unattached."

"And," Kat cut in, "she was a two-bit whore. Your friend Marci had the nasty habit of hanging out with all the wrong people."

"Suppose we drop the subject."

"On the contrary, you need to know what I learned about your little playmate. Better yet, I can show you." Kat rummaged around in her oversized purse until she found a five-by-seven envelope, opened it, and laid three snapshots on the table. "Recognize the girl? Recognize the guy?"

Seacord was stunned. "It's Marci."

"And in case you didn't recognize the man, that's the former, now-deceased, Senator from Idaho—Ben Bridgewater."

"I don't get it."

"Men." Kat sighed. "Blind as a bat unless they're looking at a pair of tits or some girl's ass. These pictures were taken at what you men like to call a smoker, over a year ago. And your friend, Marci Lincoln, attended that little affair for the sole purpose of entertaining one Senator Ben Bridgewater. Still want me to drop the subject?"

Seacord looked again at the photographs. He shook his head. "Sounds like you better keep going."

"Let's start with what I've learned so far. Remember, I'm the one that broke the story on the Bridgewater-Chen Ton affair. I saw these pictures long before that pipe bomb put an end to your little cuddle-bunny's checkered career. For the record, Marci Lincoln's real name is Dorothy Hamm and she comes from Kansas City, not Chicago. And before you protest and start telling me about her wonderful 'parents,' their real names are Art and Ruth Levitz. They're a couple of small-time con artists who have been employed on occasion by your nemesis, Chen Ton. My guess is he had them pick up her belongings because he was afraid his little hooker might have left some rather incriminating evidence lying around her apartment. Am I getting through to you yet?"

Seacord shoved the five-by-seven back across the table. "Is what you're telling me on the up and up?"

"Why the hell would I lie? It seems fairly obvious to me your little friend died because she didn't know Chen Ton's goons had rigged a pipe bomb to your phone. I've talked to the police; they tell me when she picked up that receiver, it released a tension device taped to the bottom of the table and *boom*—just like that it was all over. But just in case you haven't figured it out yet, it was supposed to be you that picked up that phone and bought the ranch. Someone was counting on that."

Seacord was still reeling. There was nothing to say and he knew it. He took a sip of his drink and shook his head. "All the same, it was a hell'uva way to go."

Kat's expression softened. "Look, I know it doesn't change what happened. The girl is dead and that's the bottom line, but at least you can stop beating yourself up now that you know who Marci Lincoln really was. She was probably the one who searched your apartment. She worked for Chen Ton and she paid the price."

Seacord finished his drink. It was turning out pretty much like he figured it would. Kat would have a whole lot to say, and he would sit there without much to say in response.

Center for Strategic Assessment
Washington
3-2

Miles Hamilton was just one of the galaxy of people Conrad Baxter had fielded calls from in his first two weeks as the new Chief Deputy Assessment Officer at the CSA. And while Baxter had quickly learned to lateral most of the calls to one of the specialists in his section, the one from Hamilton had proven to be different. Hamilton was more persistent. He had steadfastly resisted being shuffled off to one of Baxter's staff.

Now, just three days after his initial contact, the urbane representative from the International Health Organization was sitting across the desk from the one man he had heard might be able to help him.

"You'll have to forgive me, Doctor," Baxter began. "I'm new to this job and I'm still trying to learn the ropes. So far I've managed some of the tougher stuff like figuring out where the lunch room is, the latrine, and the names of about half the people on my staff. Other than that, I'm operating pretty much in the dark." He rolled Hamilton's card over in his hand, glanced at it a second time, then laid it on his desk. "So what can I do for you and the IHO?"

Miles Hamilton had the kind of prepossessing smile that made it comfortable for people to talk to him, and he capitalized on it. He cleared his throat before he began. "Well, then, suppose I start by welcoming you to Washington, Colonel, and then save us both time by getting straight to the reason for my insistence on our meeting. My colleagues at IHO are convinced that your office or someone in your organization can steer us in the right direction.

"Let me begin by saying I have recently returned from a conference in Moscow. While I was there I had an opportunity to meet with an old colleague, a Dr. Josef Chenko in the Russian Health Ministry. During that meeting, Dr. Chenko introduced me to one of his regional health officers, a young woman by the name of Dr. Rebi Chernov. And this Dr. Chernov is the reason I am here.

"It seems that on a recent inspection trip to Kirensk, a rather remote Russian military test facility, she was made aware of what appears to be a serious pollution problem. She showed me aerial photographs of an area bordering the Solonge River in northern Mongolia that indicate there has been a violent toxic reaction to something that has apparently been introduced to the river. While the area where this condition exists is sparsely populated and the impact of the pollution may at the moment be minimal, Dr. Chernov believes there is a danger of significant long-term damage. She believes that eventually there will be an even further negative impact on the environment when the polluted waters flow into Russian territory just north of the Russian-Mongolian border."

Baxter interrupted. "Forgive me, Doctor Hamilton, but my first reaction to what you are telling me is to remind you that pollution problems are somewhat outside the realm of concern of the CSA. On the other hand, I must admit that I'm curious as to why you thought the CSA might be interested."

"Under most circumstances I would agree, Colonel, it would not be your concern, but there is a twist to this that I believe will concern you. Are you aware of a supposedly defunct Chinese military installation near the Mongolian village of Kamanchu? I believe it was called the Zijin Mountain Project."

Baxter reflected back on his earlier conversation with Clark Barrows and laughed. "Actually, it's one of the few things I am familiar with, Doctor. Two, maybe three weeks ago we received reports of an underground nuclear test in the same vicinity. Our friends at the Swiss Seismological Service believe they tied a recent earthquake in that area to that test."

Hamilton's face brightened. "Then it will not be necessary for me to go into further detail. I trust your agency is investigating."

"We are," Baxter confirmed. "But I would be interested to know what else you know about the situation."

"Let's start with the fact that in the last several days I have been in touch with the appropriate officials both in Beijing and Ulan Bator in an attempt to find out what they know. Thus far I am getting very little or no cooperation. I even went so far as to offer the governments of both countries IHO assistance in helping them determine the cause of the problem. Their response was either to refuse to acknowledge there was a problem, or politely tell me it was none of my business. Which of course only makes me think they either know about the problem and are tending to it—or they are hiding something. For some reason,

I think it is the latter. Either way, I think it should concern someone."

Baxter leaned back in his chair. "So what does the IHO normally do in these kinds of situations?"

"The response of the Beijing government does not surprise us, but I was somewhat taken back by the Mongolian refusal. I received a carefully worded communique that indicated they considered it an internal matter and that they would take care of it. In my estimation, the Mongolian response amounts to a non-response. Which in turn leaves IHO with no other alternative than to seek other ways to investigate the situation."

"Maybe we should give them a little more time," Baxter suggested. "Perhaps they will do as they say."

"You do not sound particularly alarmed, Colonel," Hamilton countered. Then he paused. "It would seem to me that there is reason for more than a passive investigation. Tie an underground nuclear test into the equation, and it occurs to me that we are dealing with something perhaps slightly more insidious than simply a matter of pollution."

"You are implying what, Doctor?"

Hamilton tried smiling. If he was reading the situation correctly, his conversation with the CSA deputy had suddenly taken a wrong turn. "Forgive me if you thought I was implying something, Colonel. But the IHO views this matter as one with the potential to become a problem of significant magnitude. What I am looking for is answers—and if it comes down to it, assistance."

Baxter pressed the button on his intercom. "Jenny, see if you can locate Captain Reimers and tell him to come to my office as soon as possible." Then he looked at Hamilton. "I may not have any answers for you today, Doctor, but I believe I know how to elevate your concerns to the next level. How long will you be in Washington?"

"Frankly, Colonel, I have every intention of hanging around and pounding on doors until I can get someone to address my concerns. The situation, because of the time of year, is compounded by the fact that my colleagues and I are now convinced there may also be some sort of nuclear considerations involved. If that is the case, and there has been an accident, the situation can only be exacerbated by a further deterioration in the weather."

"I'm afraid I don't understand."

"I'm talking about cold rain, Colonel. If there has been a nuclear incident in that region, fallout is a given. Any form of precipitation, coupled with even a modest wind, can and will spread the contamination. Based on what I know now, I would have to say we are looking at a potential ecological disaster in that area."

For the first time since Conrad Baxter had accepted the position with CSA, he could feel his juices starting to flow.

IHO Headquarters
Washington
3-3

Less than twenty-four hours had passed since the initial conversation between Miles Hamilton and Conrad Baxter when they were again sitting down to discuss the matter. This time, however, the meeting was being held in a small conference room in the International Health Organization offices a few blocks down the street from G7 headquarters on 11th Street.

Following his meeting with Hamilton, Baxter had telephoned Clark Barrows and detailed the situation regarding the Russian concerns about the levels of contamination indicated in the photographs of the Solonge. Their phone conversation had been brief, but Barrows had agreed to a meeting, and assured his old friend that he would have some of his people look into the matter. As a result, Baxter, Hamilton, and Captain Reimers from the CSA were sitting across from Barrows and his administrative assistant, Chet David.

David, a six-one computer geek and workaholic, as well as being a graduate of a Virginia law school, had been Barrows's chief administrative assistant for the past thirteen years. More than any of his internal people, Chet David had become Clark Barrows's ace-in-the-hole—a logician with a penchant for detail and a memory that had been repeatedly tested and proven right. Barrows called him "the consummate digger." Now, with a stack of battered manila folders neatly arranged on the table in front of him, he was waiting for the meeting to begin and Barrows to give him the go-ahead signal.

Hamilton started with background information, and when he was finished, Barrows turned the meeting over to David.

"I thought it best to begin with a time line," he began. "Twelve years ago, the PRK was quite active in the area. There was a flurry of construction activity and we monitored the situation closely. Then, in July of 1990, an earthquake measuring 7.2 on the Richter Scale, as recorded by the Swiss Seismological team in Zurich, pretty much decimated the area. After that, construction activity was decidedly curtailed.

"Two years later a curious thing happened. The Chinese tore out their runways and much of the surface construction. Nevertheless, we continued our surveillance. Activity in the area continued, but at a greatly reduced level. For comparative purposes, I made copies of our satellite photos in both 1990 and 1994. You can see how activity diminished." David circulated the satellite images, and waited for each of the men to study them.

"I noticed that you failed to mention the fact that the Chinese built a railroad that runs from the former Kamanchu construction site to Ulan Bator," Reimers finally said.

"They did indeed," David confirmed. "And that represents one of the abnormalities of the situation at Kamanchu. That rail line was constructed long after the hydrofill dam was constructed on the Solonge River. But here's the part of it that is really difficult to understand. The railroad does not extend all the way to the dam site. It's northern terminus is some six miles from that location at Zijin Mountain. Which, of course, raises the question, if this is no longer an active military installation for the Chinese, why did they build a railroad? Plus, the rail line's termination point would seem to indicate it does not service the dam."

"Have we made any attempt to monitor personnel or supply movement?" Baxter asked.

"That's where we may have outsmarted ourselves, Colonel," David admitted. "Quite frankly, when things began heating up in the Middle East a few years back, our attention was somewhat diverted. When you called Clark yesterday, I went back to the archives and I found something rather interesting. In both 1995 and again in 1996, we recorded sporadic incidents where the rail line between Ulan Bator and Kamanchu was quite active. In those photographs it appears that the Chinese were shipping both supplies and construction equipment to what we had written off as an inactive site. Then, when CSA recently informed us that our Swiss colleagues reported an underground nuclear test in that region, it got our attention again."

"I would be interested in knowing if what you have uncovered in your research leads you to any conclusions," Baxter said.

Chet David was smiling. "Yes and no. I took the reports and satellite photos that were recorded in both 1995 and 1996 to our analysts. They believe they have identified some of the supplies on those rail flatbeds as being the possible components of a nuclear reactor. We can't be certain, of course, but the size and configuration of those components leads us in that direction."

For the first time, Hamilton spoke up. "But if the Chinese built a nuclear reactor or a missile base, wouldn't we be able to identify it from satellite photos?"

"Not if they constructed it underground," David replied. "Our people assure me that given the time and resources, they could tunnel back into one of those mountains and build one or the other, maybe both. They've got everything they need: a good way to conceal it, an abundant supply of water, and it is located in one of the most sparsely populated areas of the globe. If I wanted to hide an installation from prying eyes, frankly I can't think of a whole lot better place to do it."

"How convinced are you that the Chinese have built a nuclear reactor at Kamanchu, Mr. David?"

"I'm not. At this point it is just a theory," David admitted. "The Zijin Mountain project could be a reactor, a launch facility, or something even more insidious like a chemical weapons manufacturing plant. But based on what we know now, I would say that any suspicion about some sort of nuclear accident is likely justified."

Hamilton waited for Chet David to continue.

"In the end, though, there is only one way I know of to verify it; someone is going to have to go in there and view the situation firsthand."

"Is that possible?" Hamilton asked.

Barrows picked up his pipe. "It's possible, but also extremely risky. If someone were to be sent in there, Dr. Hamilton, they would have to disguise their real intentions. After all, both the Chinese and Mongolian authorities have made it clear that they consider the matter their own business. Then there is the matter of discovering just how toxic the situation really is. If it's as bad as you have indicated, anyone who goes in there without the proper protection will be putting their life on the line."

"There is a great deal more at stake here than the lives of a few investigators," Hamilton countered.

"When we look back at the tragedies triggered by nuclear reactor malfunctions at Chernobyl and Chelyabinsk, it becomes painfully apparent just how destructive an event of this nature can be. Having said all of that, I am curious about how you would go about investigating the facility at Kamanchu."

While Chet David listened, he continued to study the array of satellite images. Finally he spoke up. "The way I see it, if the decision is made to go into the impacted area, you'll need someone who knows the territory, preferably a local and someone we can trust. Then you'll need someone who understands the volatility of the situation and is able to identify what kinds of substances we are dealing with. Lastly, you're going to need a heavyweight, someone to do the dirty work—someone who is used to this kind of clandestine operation. If you've already had your offer of assistance turned down by both the Mongolian and Chinese governments, that tells us that anyone we send in there isn't exactly welcome. I think they've made that sufficiently clear."

Hamilton studied Barrows's placid face for several moments before he posed his next question. "Suppose for a moment that the IHO were to make an official request for assistance through the proper authorities. How long would it take to obtain the right agency's blessing and put a team together?"

Hamilton was confident he understood the ponderous pace of bureaucracy as well as anyone in the room, and he realized that such a request would require approval upon approval. Still, he was uncertain whether or not Barrows and his assistant understood just how urgent the matter was becoming.

"Just how familiar are you with the mission of G7, Doctor?" Barrows asked.

"To be quite honest, Mr. Barrows, I had never even heard of G7 until Colonel Baxter suggested that we meet."

"That's the way we would prefer it," Barrows admitted. "Anonymity in our line of work has distinct advantages. Let me explain it this way. We are very much like our more highly publicized colleagues, the Navy SEALs. The difference, of course, is that for the most part we wear business suits instead of wet suits. But we, too, do what has to be done and worry about explaining it later."

"Then you are saying a covert mission is a distinct possibility?"

"As long as I keep the boss informed."

"You are referring to—"

"Let's just say we have a conduit to some people in high places, Dr. Hamilton." Barrows's expression revealed nothing. "Give me twenty-four to forty-eight hours to put some kind of plan together, talk to a few people, and get back to you. I trust your situation in Kamanchu will not go away in that amount of time."

"Anything you can do to push it through channels will be appreciated," Hamilton said.

For Seacord it had been a long week, but finally the doctors had given him clearance to return to duty. He had attempted to celebrate by taking his long-neglected morning jog, called his daughter in Key West to inform her of the good news, and finished his morning by stopping by his condominium to see how much progress was being made on repairs. The condo, freshly painted and recarpeted, was almost ready.

After that, he had lunch at the Air Force Club, checked his mail, and even entertained, albeit it briefly, the thought of stopping at the Chinese embassy to confront Chen Ton. In the end, good judgment prevailed and he instead drove to G7 headquarters.

The doctor had advised him to take it slow and easy for the first few days, and by mid-afternoon he found himself in the parking lot outside the nondescript building, feeling listless and worn out. He was beginning to understand why they called it a recuperation period.

Inside, he shrugged off a bevy of questions about how he was feeling, and made his way to Clark Barrows's office. There, the G7 director wasted no time bringing him up to speed on agency affairs. Ten minutes later they were into what Barrows was calling the "Kirensk matter." Seacord was still poring over satellite images and digesting Chet David's typed notes from the meeting with Hamilton and the people from CSA when Barrows began asking questions.

"Off the top of your head, T. J., what's your first reaction?"

"I'd say it has all the ingredients of a king-size speed bump, Clark. David's theory that the Chinese may have built something as deadly as a bio-warfare plant or nuclear reactor in the middle of that mountain, plus the rail spur, personnel movements, supply shipments, and now this, all point to something nasty. That part of the world is pretty damn remote. Maybe they're dumping their nuclear waste materials in the river. Maybe they think it doesn't matter."

"It's hard for me to believe they would be that foolish," Barrows said. "They'd have to figure someone would take notice and start asking questions. If they are trying to keep this installation a secret, dumping something in a river that's going to defoliate the countryside is bound to raise a few questions. I think it's more likely that they have experienced a problem of some kind."

"A meltdown?"

"Not necessarily."

"What has David come up with so far?"

"At this point mostly background information. Even if there was a meltdown and that's what those explosions were, they've built the reactor inside the mountain to conceal it. It stands to reason they are counting on the interior of that mountain to serve as the containment unit. Reactor failure isn't the only possibility, though. The defoliation could be the result of several other possibilities."

For the first time in weeks Seacord was beginning to feel useful. Finally he was doing something. It felt good. "It's been a long time since I've been involved with anything of this nature, but as I recall, there are two things that could cause a reactor to fail, loss of coolant or any one of several what they call 'transient' conditions."

" 'Transient' conditions could mean almost anything," Barrows reminded him. "Bottom line, we've uncovered a nasty little secret and the first-blush thinking is it's going to get worse before it gets fixed. Couple that with the fact that Hamilton indicates he's getting no cooperation from either the Chinese or the

Mongolians, and we've got a disagreeable situation on our hands. Most certainly one that everyone would like to keep in the family."

"So what's the bottom, bottom line."

"The IHO wants us to help them find a way to investigate, and I'm inclined to tell Hamilton we'll give it a shot. I've spent most of the afternoon thinking about how we would go about it and who we would send. The name that keeps popping up is Vincent Rubbra. Think he could handle it?"

Seacord hedged, indicating he wasn't familiar enough with Rubbra's fitness report to comment one way or the other. "Why Rubbra?"

Barrows enumerated. "One, he is familiar with Ulan Bator. Two, he speaks Russian fluently. Three, he isn't currently on assignment." With that Barrows paused. "In the end, though, it will be up to Hamilton. It's his show and as recently as our phone conversation two hours ago, he said he was convinced the Russians would want to play a role in any action we take."

Seacord frowned. "Under what guise?"

"That's the part I haven't figured out yet," Barrows admitted. "Right now, Chet David may have the best idea. He thinks we should put a team together and go in flying the IHO colors. He envisions a hit-and-run operation. Get in, get out. Then let the world know what we uncovered. If we should happen to get caught, we can always hide behind the IHO flag."

Seacord was in agreement. "Sounds solid. So what's your next move?"

"I've got a call into Harry Driver. I don't want to

take it any farther until I know we've got the Main Man's blessing."

"How long will that take?"

"I'll know after I talk to Driver."

Thirty minutes after his session with Barrows, Seacord spent another hour with Chet David reviewing the Chen Ton files and waiting for the afternoon's rush hour traffic to thin out. The two men spent most of their time going over the information David had obtained from various sources on the progress of the Bridgewater investigation. After listening, Seacord decided that neither the Washington police nor the two government agencies involved had made any real progress. David's assessment of the situation was similar. The police were no closer to identifying Bridgewater's killer than they had been before the pipe bomb incident in Seacord's condominium.

It was now known, however, that Dorothy Hamm, alias Marci Lincoln, had been seen frequently with Senator Bridgewater prior to his death. As Kat had claimed, the fact that she also had ties to Chen Ton was a matter of record. The net was tightening, but there was still nothing to directly tie Chen Ton to the Senator's murder. All that police knew for certain was that someone had shoved a six-inch blade into Bridgewater's ribs and left him to die in a service elevator at the Grand Mark Hotel. The murder had occurred less than a month before the Senate was scheduled to open hearings on the relationship between Bridgewater and his friends at the Chinese embassy. Everything else, they claimed, came under the heading of circumstantial evidence.

Everyone was aware that Seacord had been the

only other person in that Macao hotel room the night Chen Ton bragged he was the one who had engineered Bridgewater's death. There were no witnesses to either the murder or the Seacord-Chen Ton conversations. It boiled down to Chen Ton's word against those of his accusers. "And two of the three witnesses who claim they knew and could prove Chen Ton was behind the Senator's death are either long gone or confirmed dead," David reminded him.

As far as Seacord was concerned, it was beginning to look like Chen Ton was right. He had boasted he would never be indicted because he knew the right people in the right places and enjoyed diplomatic immunity. If there wasn't a break in the case soon, Chen Ton was going to get away with the murder of a United States Senator.

It was nearly six-thirty and most of the day staff had departed when Chet David began stuffing papers back in their folders and locking them in the files.

"That's enough for one day," he grumbled. "Besides, you look like you need a little fortification. How about grabbing something to eat?"

Seacord was ready for it. "You're on," he said. "I know a place where they make the mother of all corn beef sandwiches and the beer is cold enough to frost your dingus. How about it?"

Chet David was all smiles. "You're the man. You lead, I'll follow."

Some twenty-five minutes later, after wending his way through a maze of Washington traffic, Seacord squeezed into the crowded parking lot of the Green Frog. It was the first time he had been there since the night Kat told him the truth about Marci. Thursday nights were usually busy, but it wasn't until he opened his car door and started to get out that he realized not everyone was there for the corn beef or to listen to the girl in the tight white dress. There were two of them; they looked like trouble and it didn't take them long to prove that they were. They emerged from the lengthening shadows between parked cars and didn't waste time on formalities. The big one landed the first blow, and he landed it where it would do the most damage. Seacord felt the air explode out of him and a sharp pain scream up his spine and slam into the base of his brain. He reeled backward and collided with the side of his car.

He spent the next several seconds trying to suck air back into his lungs, and when it didn't happen, he realized just how much trouble he was in.

The second blow was a karate chop that caught him in the throat. This time his knees went rubbery, his world became instantly fuzzy, and he started seeking the sanctuary of lower ground. But before he could get that far, the big guy had jerked him to his feet again and deftly administered two sledgehammer blows to his still-tender face. Seacord's mouth flooded with the taste of salty blood and his vision refused to track. He felt two ham-sized hands encircle his neck, the fingers lock, and his attacker jerk down just as he brought his knee up. The effect was potent. He heard the sickening sound of himself splintering.

He dropped to his knees again, tried to cover his face and prepare for the next attack. This time it wasn't a fist—it was the cold, hard muzzle of a snub-nosed revolver. One of his new playmates had unceremoniously jammed it into the fleshy part of his throat.

Seacord tried shaking his head in what turned out to be an ill-conceived attempt to clear his vision. The gesture did nothing more then intensify the pain, and his world got darker while his stomach started doing cartwheels. Contrary to what felt like the devastating attack of an entire goon platoon, it had taken only one of them to do the damage. Either the big guy's partner wasn't in the mood, or he hadn't seen fit to get involved in the rough stuff up until the moment when he thought Seacord was ready.

As T. J. was yanked to his feet a second time and slammed backward against the hood of his car, the big man's backup finally decided to get involved. Unlike his partner, Number Two didn't pound; he wheezed what he had to say.

"You know somethin', cowboy, the boss thinks you're becoming a major-league pain in the ass. He says you hang out with the wrong people and that's startin' to annoy him."

Seacord could hear the man, and he was somehow able to decipher most of what he was saying, but the rest of his senses were a blur. When he tried to reply, the words ended up sideways, trapped in his throat, never quite making it out. Damage control had taken over, and his brain was sending out a series of semi-coherent, half-muted signals that were telling him to keep his mouth shut.

The man with the gun said, "This time we do the talkin', cowboy. Got it? We talk. You listen." Number One spun him around, pinning him against the side of his car while Seacord was still trying to clear his head. "We think you oughta know somethin'. We done our homework and we learned somethin' real important-like. A couple of weeks ago, you spent a little time in Key West. Big mistake, cowboy. 'Cause now we know about your daughter. If you keep gettin' in the way, that daughter of yours will get that pretty little face of hers splattered all over Alvera Street. Got it?"

Seacord figured at that point some sort of signal passed between his two assailants, because the little guy stepped away and his bulldog friend took over again. He delivered a couple of quick punches to Seacord's midsection, followed up with a well-placed knee to his crotch, and Seacord's lights began to flicker. He slowly crumpled to the blacktop while his world went spinning off into alien orbits. At that point there was only a partial awareness on his part that his newfound playmates had grown tired of pounding on him. The last thing he remembered was the sound of hurried footsteps fading into what had become a very unpleasant and surrealistic nightmare. The world was pressing down on him and something else was closing his eyes. He was hoping against hope that the feeble gesture would shut out the pain and nausea.

1910 High Terrace
Ravenwood, Virginia
3-4

Seacord had once heard that the return to consciousness was similar to that of emerging from the womb. While he couldn't recall his birth, if it was anything like what he was currently experiencing, he sure as hell knew it wasn't an experience he wanted to relive.

First he became aware of sounds—tempered, meaningless, discordant. Then there was the presence of a different kind of light, not the disorienting glare that had been probing around in his brain, but an unknown source of illumination where half-shadows and vague images prevailed. He opened his eyes, discovered that everything was still throbbing, and closed them again. From somewhere in the tortured mass of tissue he called a brain, he was getting a signal; it was telling him to deal with one thing at a time. He kept his eyes closed and listened. When he did, it was only the voice he had to decipher. One, it was that of a woman. Two, she sounded vaguely familiar. Three, she did not sound threatening. Based on that, he tried opening his eyes again.

"I think he's starting to come around." This time it was a man's voice. Like the woman's, this one sounded more concerned than hostile, and he tried to articulate some kind of response, only to learn the effort was futile. Whatever was in there wasn't coming out.

"It's okay, T. J.," he heard Mary say. "Lay still. Rest. You're safe."

Now the voice was Clark's. Unlike their conversation earlier in his office, now the tone of the man's voice was solicitous; there was no edge, no expectation to it.

"Chet found you in the parking lot. He stuffed you in his car, called me, and brought you here. We didn't take you to the emergency room because we thought it best to keep this whole incident under wraps until we knew exactly what happened. Was it Chen Ton's people?"

Seacord tried to nod, but the gesture was painful. "I . . . I think so . . . ," he finally managed. His voice was weak, his words garbled.

He saw Barrows glance at his wife before his friend continued. "I've called a doctor friend of mine. He's coming over to take a look at you. In the meantime, do what you can to rest."

Thomas Jefferson Seacord didn't need encouragement. He closed his eyes and within moments had again spiraled into oblivion.

Chet David glanced at the clock in the Barrowses' kitchen and yawned. It was two-thirty, several hours later than when he usually called it a day. Behind him, Clark was playing with the dials on the television when Mary and the doctor walked out of the spare bedroom. "I guess it's good news," she said. "Doctor Goodman says T. J. looks and probably feels a whole lot worse than he actually is."

"I gave him a sedative," Goodman volunteered. "At this point your friend in there needs sleep more than he needs a doctor."

Kenneth Goodman, a stocky little man with a pencil-thin mustache, had been the Barrows family doctor for as long as either of them could remember. In addition, they were close enough personally that Clark felt comfortable asking him to make a house call. Now, as Goodman accepted Mary's offer of coffee and sat down, he looked bewildered.

"Look, I don't know what's going on here, Clark,

but you could have taken your friend in there to any emergency room in the area and they would have had him fixed up in no time."

"There's a reason, Ken. I'll explain later."

Goodman took a sip of coffee and set his cup down. "Mary is right. They roughed him pretty good. Still, I couldn't find anything that would indicate he suffered any permanent damage. We may have to re-arrange his face at some point; his nose is broken and he is going to find it hard to chew for a while. My guess is they knew what they were doing, because it could have been a whole lot worse. They could have split his head open. It seems fairly obvious, though, that they knew when to stop. Like I say, his face is pretty well chopped up, but Mary tells me your friend in there is the same one that had a pipe bomb go off in his condo a couple of weeks ago. If he were a friend of mine I'd give him a little advice. I'd tell him to get some new friends and stay away from the Green Frog."

For the first time since Chet David's call, Clark and Mary Barrows both breathed a sigh of relief. "How long before he's up and around?" Clark asked.

"It all depends on how he feels. My guess is he won't feel like doing much tomorrow. Maybe the next day. Either way he'll be sore as hell for a while."

Barrows was hedging. He looked uneasy. "Now comes the sixty-four-dollar question, Doc. Is there anything in all of this that you or I have to report?"

Goodman was puzzled. "That's the procedure. Why? Is there something here I'm missing?"

"We've been friends a long time, Ken, and I don't want to ask you to do anything that would break any laws or violate any oaths. But this gets fairly involved, and I'm asking you to trust me until we can figure out how we want to handle it."

Barrows could tell by the expression on his friend's face that he did not understand. "In other words you *don't* want me to report this and you don't intend to either," said Goodman. "Am I reading you right?"

Barrows nodded. "I don't ask you about your work and you don't ask me about mine."

Goodman finished his coffee. He was still frowning as he stood up and looked at Mary. "Come to think of it, Clark, I don't even know this guy's name. How's that?"

He had been gone for several minutes when Mary spoke up. "Why wouldn't you let Ken report it?"

"Right now we don't have any proof that Chen Ton was behind all of this. Chet is right. This was supposed to look like a mugging, nothing more. They took T. J.'s wallet, his watch, and everything else of value."

"I still don't understand," Mary persisted.

"You will when I get all the pieces put together."

Office of Harry Driver
White House
3-5

The media and most everyone in Washington that wasn't close to the Norris Administration had names for Harry Elsworth Driver, none of which were complimentary. Administration insiders knew a different Driver, and they knew that when historians finally got around to chronicling the accomplishments and foibles of Norris's terms in office, readers would learn what Driver had brought to the table.

Harry Driver operated in the world of government secrets and shadows. He did the dirty work and he seemed to enjoy it. It was his job not only to cover the President's backside, but to monitor cloakroom whisperings, street talk, and rumors. In the secret world of Harry Driver, there was no applause or accolades. He was a night messenger, a cover-up artist, and when necessary, the Machiavellian mind in Norris's court. In the White House phone book he was listed as a Presidential Aide, but the title, as far as most people were concerned, was a misnomer. He was a roadblock, a strainer, a hurdle, and a truth seeker.

To Barrows, Driver was a hardheaded logician, a former Marine who before he had shaved his head, had still worn his hair "high and tight." He had penetrating brown-black eyes and a curt, decidedly uncourtly manner that more often than not offended his contacts. His only concession to protocol was the fact that he maintained an office in a small room adjacent to the ground-floor library. The room contained a metal desk, three chairs, a brace of file cabinets, two phones, two computers, and two televisions. He was the only one who had a key. When he had meetings with the Clark Barrowses of the world, he conducted the entire session like a homicide interrogation.

Now, with both Barrows and Chet David sitting

across from him in the tiny room, he was trying to assess the reams of information the G7 DDO and his assistant had covered in the last two hours. Chet David had done his usual thorough job—if for no other reason than over the years he had learned to anticipate Driver's questions. David had provided Driver with a roster of names, several detailed maps, and seven pages of computer printouts with key dates and facts.

During the course of the two-hour briefing, Driver had interrupted the proceedings to make two telephone calls: one to check on the President's itinerary, and the second to check on the availability of the President for a brief meeting.

"The only thing you left out," Driver finally grunted, "is who you intend to send with the IHO representative and how you intend to disguise this little charade of yours."

"Keep in mind the Russians want a piece of this one," Barrows reminded him. "They're the ones that made the appeal to the IHO through Miles Hamilton. It sounds to me like they are more than eager to blow the whistle on the Chinese. At the same time they also are the ones who have the most to lose if they make a big stink about it and this Dr. Chernov's assessment of the situation turns out to be incorrect."

Driver lit a cigarette and frowned as Barrows continued. "Go on."

"The obvious next question then is, why are they asking for our assistance? The answer is, according to Hamilton the Russian health officials have run into a stone wall at the Kremlin. Hamilton is convinced any effort mounted by the Russian health authorities alone will be turned back at the border."

"Sounds messy," Driver agreed. "You know damn well what the President's first question is going to be. He's going to want to know what we have to gain by being willing to put our own tit in this wringer."

It was the question Barrows had been waiting for. "Tell him everything points to the fact that the Chinese have been building and testing some type of nuclear device in the area. Less than a month ago the Swiss Seismological people in Zurich reported recording an underground nuclear explosion in that very area. Our best information up until recently has led us to believe that the Chinese closed down their Zijin Mountain base at Kamanchu several years ago. But the detonation of some sort of nuclear device in that region makes us think maybe they have reactivated it."

"Or that they have built their facility in the side of the mountain so that we can't get pictures of it," David added. "The way we see it, by cooperating with the IHO, we build a little goodwill by helping the Russians discover the source of the pollution. And at the same time we use this as an opportunity to find out what the Chinese have up their sleeve. This is one of those times when the right hand doesn't necessarily have to know what the left hand is doing."

Driver continued to frown. "So you're proposing sending in one of your people with an IHO team composed of . . ."

"We haven't worked out all the details yet. What

we're trying to sell is the concept. Who goes, who stays, that's Hamilton's call. But he came to us for help. It's up to us to find a way to get him and the rest of the team in there to have a look around, determine the cause of the pollution, and while we're at it, find out what's going on at Kamanchu."

Even before Barrow had finished, Driver began shaking his head. "Who in the hell over at G7 comes up with these half-assed schemes. I'll be up front with you on this one, Clark; I don't like the sound of it. What makes you think we have any better chance of pulling this off than the Russians? What's to stop them from going in and conducting their own secret investigation? They sure as hell know the territory better than we do."

"Like I said, the Kremlin has already said 'no way.' But getting the IHO involved puts a whole different spin on it. Without our help they get stopped at the border. We are confident we can find a way to get across that border, do what we have to do, and get out before anyone knows we're even there."

Driver pushed his chair back and closed the file. He was still frowning. "This one isn't my call," he admitted. "I'll talk to the Main Man, but if he asks me what I think, I'll have to tell him I don't like the sound of it."

David waited. He knew Barrows wasn't through trying to sell his plan. The G7 chief opened his briefcase, took out a sealed envelope, and slid it across the desk. "The President will want to know about this."

"And this pertains to what?" Driver pushed.

Barrows smiled. "Well, now, Harry, it's like this. If I wanted anyone beside the President to know what's in that envelope, I wouldn't have sealed it, would I?"

Chapter Four

Building 231
Washington
4-1

Following their nearly three-hour session with Harry Driver, Clark Barrows and Chet David returned to the G7 offices to put the first phase of the plan into gear. Barrows returned several phone calls, the most important being to Miles Hamilton. He informed the IHO representative that "the appropriate authorities" had been brought up to date on the situation in Kamanchu, and had promised a "go" or "no go" decision within a matter of hours. Before he hung up, he informed Hamilton he expected a decision that day.

Meanwhile, Chet David began the arduous task of pulling together the materials a G7 agent would need to accompany the IHO team if Barrows's plan was approved.

While Barrows and David were putting the first phase of the plan in gear, Clark's wife was carefully following her husband's instructions. She was transporting Seacord to a scheduled six-thirty meeting at the 231 building. "Whatever you do," Barrows had warned her; "keep T. J. out of sight. Use the rear entrance. I've tipped off the security people. They will meet you at the gate and they will take it from there. They will use the rear entrance and the service elevator to get him to the conference room on the third floor. If we're going to pull this charade off, it's imperative no one knows T. J. is in the building."

Mary Barrows was smiling. She was pleased with herself. It wasn't the first time she had been asked to assist her husband with an agency matter, but she could not remember when he had been so explicit. She delivered T. J. to the appointed place at the appointed time, rendezvoused with the security team, handed Seacord over, and drove off intent on keeping a dinnertime hair appointment. Most impressive of all, she had avoided revealing any of the details of the convoluted scheme her husband and Chet David had worked out at the Barrowses' kitchen table the night before.

Now, with Seacord sitting across the desk from him, Barrows was wasting no time getting started. "I've asked Vince Rubbra to join us, T. J., because there has been a slight change in plans. Instead of sending Rubbra with whoever the IHO people put together, we are sending you. Vince will be your backup in the event the AG breaks something on the Chen Ton matter in the next forty-eight hours."

"Send me where?"

"I'll get to that. As an added precaution, we've also decided to put Vince through the 'make ready' drill right along with you. But before he gets here, I want to give you some idea of what else we've put together in the last twenty-four hours.

"First of all, let me put your mind at ease about Lucy. Mary overheard you when you called her last night. We know about the threat. To defuse that situation, at two o'clock this afternoon, Mark Garfield, our agent in Miami, hustled her out of Key West and boarded a plane with her to Boston. As far as Chen Ton's people are concerned, if and when they actually do go looking for her, she will have disappeared from the face of the earth. Only our people know where she is, and all of them are trustworthy. Chen won't be able to dig it out of any influential friends. Okay."

Seacord breathed easier.

"Now, on to other matters. If all goes as planned, at ten o'clock tonight, under what will appear to be a veil of secrecy, you will be admitted to the ICU at Saint Francis Hospital. There you will be guarded night and day until the Attorney General gives us the all-clear."

Seacord was stunned. "Hospital? What the hell for? Outside of a few bumps and bruises, I'll be ready to go back to work in a couple of days."

Barrows held up his hand. "Relax. Wait until I've

finished. Our story is going to be that you are in critical condition. No one will be allowed to see or talk to you other than approved members of the staff at the hospital. So far I've got the cooperation of the Attorney General, the Washington police, and the hospital administration on this one. The AG, Chet, and I, along with three of our agents acting as your private duty nurses, are the only ones that will know it's not actually you in that room."

Seacord was still frowning. "If I'm not in that room, Clark, I've got to be somewhere—"

Barrows was enjoying himself. "If you're in Kamanchu, you're going to be a long, long way from that hospital. You can thank Chet for this one. We've been trying to figure out the best way to handle a situation that has arisen with the IHO, and we're convinced you're the solution. You're going to be part of the contingent the IHO is getting ready to send to Kamanchu. As soon as we can get you briefed, you'll be accompanying someone from the IHO along with the Russian representative into Kamanchu to investigate a situation there.

"When we informed the Attorney General about the second attack and the threat on your daughter, he advised us to keep you under wraps and hide Lucy. So, that's exactly what we're doing. Chet and I figure that halfway around the globe ought to be far enough away to keep Chen Ton's people off your back.

"Like I said, as a precaution we intend to put Vince through the briefing right along with you. He'll go only if you're needed here. As long as you're healthy enough to get on the plane when it leaves for Moscow on Saturday, you're the man."

"What about the Bridgewater investigation?"

"The Attorney General thinks he needs a minimum of another two to three weeks to get his ducks lined up. According to the AG, Chen Ton is up to his ass in alligators in more ways than one. Between the Bridgewater affair and what the AG has uncovered in the last forty-eight hours, he's convinced if he has time to prepare his case, he can take Chen out of circulation permanently. But, he says he isn't ready yet. In any case, even if you were here, you wouldn't be expected to testify again until they bring him to trial."

Seacord was listening, but he was wondering if Barrows realized he needed a couple of more days, perhaps longer, to get his act together. His face looked like dough, and at the moment he was unable to even shift his weight in a chair without something hurting. All of which was making him question what kind of contribution he could make to an expedition tromping through northern Mongolia. Still, at that particular moment, he was even more concerned about Lucy. Getting her out of Key West was one thing; hiding her from Chen Ton's people was another.

He was still trying to put Lucy out of his mind when he asked, "So, when do we start putting this little charade of yours together?"

"If you think you're ready, we'll get started now. We've got a lot to accomplish and not a lot of time to do it. Now comes the key question. Do you think you're up to it?"

Seacord winced. Even so, he heard himself saying, "What the hell, I guess I don't have anything better to do."

* * *

For Thomas Jefferson Seacord, it was his first encounter with the man referred to by the rest of the agency as the "Ice Man." Rubbra hailed from Kenya. At first sight, the man reliable sources claimed had once snapped the neck of a would-be Presidential assassin in his country with his bare hands, was less than imposing. He was slight in build, with small features and an implacable exterior.

He shook hands with Seacord as the two men were being introduced, but even then Rubbra conveyed the demeanor of a man who was cold and impersonal.

Up until that moment, all Seacord had known about Rubbra was what he had heard and what he had read in the agency fitness reports. Vincent Agapar Rubbra had earned a degree while studying at Colgate, and had been with the agency for ten years now. Those who knew him acknowledged his brilliance, but they were equally quick to confirm his reputation for being morose and a loner.

As Seacord studied the man Barrows had designated as his backup, he decided Rubbra's complexion was the closest thing to polished ebony he had ever seen. The color of his skin was in complete harmony with his doll-like eyes: cold, black, and devoid of expression.

"Welcome to Arcania 101." Seacord grinned.

Rubbra acknowledged him with a barely perceptible nod. He made no other attempt at a response.

"If you will be seated, gentlemen," Barrows began, "we can get started."

It was SOP for Barrows to devote the first five or ten minutes of any briefing to a review of the problem. Then, as satellite photos were passed around, he began to unfold the intricacies of his plan. "Any moment now I'm expecting a call from Harry Driver. Obviously I'm anticipating that the President has given his blessing to all this. When that happens, T. J., you'll think you're back in school. Between Chet and me, it's our intention to cram as much information into you and Vincent as you two can assimilate in the next two days. To start with, you'll each be given a new identity. We also intend to teach you two everything we can about nuclear reactors, nuclear weapons, the effects of radiation poisoning, and enough medical jargon to make you sound like you know what you're talking about.

"IHO concerns notwithstanding, the assumption in all of this is that our Chinese friends have been busy building a nuclear reactor, or developing nuclear weapons, or conducting nuclear weapons tests somewhere in the area around Kamanchu. If that's the case, we want to know how much, when, what kind of device, and more important, what they plan to do with it. If everything goes according to schedule, T. J., you'll be on a plane to Moscow early Saturday morning along with the representative of the IHO. When you get to Moscow, you will meet whomever the Russians decide to put on the team."

When Barrows paused, Chet David asked, "Any questions so far?"

Seacord shook his head and Barrows continued. "Finally—and I don't think it is necessary to belabor this at this point, T. J.—but you realize of course that you will have an additional assignment. We are cooperating with the IHO and the Russians because we think it is important to help them determine the source and magnitude of the pollution. That much is a given. At the same time, we think it is equally important that something be done about that source when we find it. What, of course, depends on what you find when you get there. Have I made myself clear on that point?"

Seacord nodded. "Let's talk about what you haven't covered, Clark. What do we know about the Russian contingent? Who are they and how many will be going in with our so-called IHO team?"

Barrows shook his head. "Unknown at this time; the same goes for the IHO representative that will be accompanying you. I can tell you this much. This Dr. Chernov that discovered the problem is a woman." He paused, then added, "And just for the record, Hamilton says she is not only bright, she is extremely attractive."

1910 High Terrace
Ravenwood, Virginia
4-2

By ten-thirty that evening Clark Barrows had finally received the call for which he had been waiting. "You have your authorization," Driver grunted. He sounded surly. "But the President stressed he wants to be kept up to date. As it turns out, you and your friends at IHO win the prize for piss-poor timing. Your little junket just happens to coincide with a visit by Premier Chang of China. Reading between the lines that means, if this thing falls apart and embarrasses us, Norris says he'll have your head on a goddamn platter."

Clark was relieved. He knew that Harry was one of the President's closest advisors and that the ex-Marine had no doubt counseled the President to veto the idea. But in the end Driver had delivered the message just as Barrows had presented it. That was what made him valuable.

"I owe you one," Barrows said. "I'll go to bat for you on one of your screwball schemes some day."

"Fat chance. Just keep in mind the Man says you better find some place to hide if this situation gets fucked up." With that, Driver hung up, but not before reminding Barrows he expected updates every twenty-four hours.

Barrows shifted the receiver from one hand to another without bothering to hang up, and dialed his assistant. This time the conversation sounded even more cryptic. "Everything in place?"

David was equally sparse with his words. "We moved into the hospital room less than ten minutes ago. There's a guard at the door as we speak. I've been assured they'll be there around the clock." Then he added, "You should have seen the looks on the faces of the night shift around here when we wheeled that gurney in with a shroud around it. This place is buzzing. They may be used to this kind of thing at Walter Reed, but apparently not here." Then David paused again. "Better brace yourself, Chief. In another ten minutes or so the switchboard down at headquarters is going to start lighting up like a cheap pinball machine. When they don't get answers at 231, they're bound to start calling you."

Clark Barrows knew what to expect. He grunted, nestled the receiver back in the cradle, looked around the room, and reached for his coffee. "So far, so good. Shall we go in and turn on the television? Let's see how long it takes them to get it on the air."

The first phone call came just as Chet David had predicted it would—some twenty-seven minutes after Barrows had hung up. It was Harry Driver again. "Clark, I'm in the car, headed home, listening to the news; what's this about Seacord? They say he's in the IC unit at Saint Francis Hospital. What the hell happened?"

Barrows had rehearsed it. "Chen Ton's people clubbed him around in the parking lot of the Green Frog. They roughed him up pretty good, mostly head injuries."

"Why the hell didn't you say something when you were in my office today?"

"The Attorney General wanted it kept quiet. We were supposed to keep a lid on it, but apparently someone at the hospital leaked it."

Barrows could tell Driver was still digesting what he had just heard. There was an uneasy silence on the other end of the line before Driver continued. "What's the prognosis?"

"At the moment there is no prognosis. No visitors, no phone calls, no nothing. They'll run more tests tomorrow. They're worried it's a blood clot on the brain. This is the second time someone has tried to make certain T. J. doesn't testify about Chen Ton's boasts while they were locked up in that hotel room in Macao."

Harry Driver was an old pro, and had been around long enough to know this was neither the time nor the place to press for answers. He knew Clark Barrows well enough to know that for the moment, the G7 DDO had told him everything he was going to. Finally he said, "Keep me informed, okay? And if you do get a chance to talk to T. J., tell him we're rooting for him."

Before Barrows could respond, he heard the sound of the disconnect. He hung up and looked across the room toward both his wife and Seacord. "Well, one down; how many to go? Did I sound convincing? Or should I do some more practicing?"

Less than five minutes later he got the one call he was dreading. It was Kat, and she sounded justifiably distraught. Manipulating the facts with Driver was part of the job. It came easy. Sometimes too easy. When that happened, Clark Barrows felt a tinge of guilt. Convincing Kat Collins was going to be a great deal more difficult. Even if he succeeded, he knew he would be feeling more than just a tinge.

"Why didn't you call me?" she asked, obviously on the verge of losing control. "I walked into the copy room a few moments ago and someone handed me a note. It said Thomas had been admitted to Saint Francis Hospital. I didn't even know he had been injured."

Barrows struggled to keep his voice steady. Dealing with Kat would be difficult for he knew Seacord would not want her to worry. He was tempted to tell her about the scheme that he and Chet had dreamed up with the help of the Attorney General, but he knew better. The more people who knew what was really happening, the more likely it was that the cover would be blown. He measured his words carefully, taking her step by step through the last forty-eight hours, detailing Seacord's injuries and emphasizing the Attorney General's insistence that no one—he stressed the words *no one*—be allowed in T. J.'s room.

"When can I see him?" Kat demanded.

"When the Attorney General says no one, Kat, he means no one. First of all, they don't know the extent of his injuries as of yet. That's why they'll be running more tests in the morning. Secondly, hospital security has been stepped up. They are determined to make certain no one goes in or out of that IC unit except authorized hospital personnel."

"For God's sake, Clark, I'm his wife."

"Ex-wife," Barrows reminded. "Hell, Kat, they won't even let *me* in."

"That's a fucking lie, Clark, and you know it." Kat Collins could snarl when she wanted to . . . and it was obvious she wanted to.

"Look. All I can tell you is T. J. is safe. Don't worry, he's in good hands, completely isolated, and he's getting the best care possible."

"Damn it, Clark, you could get me in there if you tried."

"I'm sorry." Barrows knew the apology sounded hollow, but under the circumstances it was all he could think to say. He knew Seacord's ex-wife well enough to know that between her anger at being shut out and her concern for T. J., she couldn't decide whether to cry or lash out with a string of profanity.

"How will I know what's happening?" she pressed.

"When I know something, you'll know something," he assured her.

"Promise me you'll call me the minute you hear anything."

"You have my word," Barrows said. When he finally hung up, he took a deep breath. "The rest of this little charade should be a piece of cake after that."

Building 231
Washington
4-3

For Seacord and Rubbra it was mid-afternoon of the second day of what Clark Barrows was describing as the mother of all crash courses in deception. Things were happening fast. Seacord had been given a name and credentials to support his new identity. In a matter of a handful of hours he had undergone what G7 considered a level-one transformation. Thomas Jefferson Seacord was now Dr. Quentin Shell, a specialist in Sino-Mongolian affairs from the University of Pennsylvania. Passports, photographs, and papers were doctored, duly aged, and appropriately validated. In typical Chet David fashion, Barrows's assistant had even gone so far as to have articles in academic journals removed, altered to show they had been authored by Shell, and then reinserted.

Now Seacord, with Rubbra accompanying him each step of the way, listened to one Dr. Glenna Bertram, a specialist in the field of radiation effects brought in by Barrows. Bertram knew only that it was her responsibility to review the subject of a variety of radiation effects. She had not been told why. To her credit, the woman was methodical and thorough; Seacord was grateful. "Mr. Barrows has indicated that based on the information the agency has obtained so far, anyone who goes into the impacted area is likely to discover cases of acute radiation effects. If that is the case, you should know that high whole-body exposure to radiation usually produces a characteristic pattern of affliction and impairment.

"Massive doses, such as those experienced in a nuclear accident of considerable magnitude, severely damage the human vascular system. This most certainly will cause cerebral edema, and death will usually occur within forty-eight hours.

"Lesser doses, something less than four thousand rads, will generally result in death in less than ten days. Any dose up to one thousand rads will probably result in some sort of infection or internal bleeding. At this level, the dosage takes a bit longer to be fatal. In this latter instance you may be looking at life expectancy of no more than four, possibly five weeks at the very most."

Seacord continued to take notes. "Based on the few photographs you've seen, Dr. Bertram, are we looking at what you would consider a serious situation?"

"It would appear to be, but until you investigate there is no way of knowing for certain. However, from what Mr. Barrows has described and based on the photographs I've seen, I believe the area in question received large doses of radiation in a short amount of time. Repair of tissue is less likely when that happens. Damage to tissue leads to damage of blood vessels. The result is malfunction of organs and necrosis, hence tissue death and, predictably, gangrene." Then she added, "It all happens quite rapidly."

Seacord picked up his voice recorder, checked the tape, glanced back through his notes, and waited for the woman to continue. Instead of continuing, she asked a question. "Are you aware that you are going into a part of the world where radioactive contamination is considered to be the number-one environmental problem?"

Seacord shook his head. "I was hoping you weren't going to say something like that," he said.

Bertram smiled. "Statistics show that four out of every five inhabitants in the impacted area are likely to be chronically ill or dying. Plus, we don't really know the impact on those areas immediately adjacent to the impinged area. It too could be quite devastating. Keep in mind that winds and, particularly, any form of precipitation are your biggest enemies; they scatter radioactivity. There is a strong likelihood that a large percentage of the people you come in contact with in the impacted area are likely to be invalids, suffering from chronic headaches, internal bleeding, anemia, even leukemia. It will not," she concluded, "be a pretty picture."

As Bertram began gathering up her papers, she looked at Seacord. "Do you have any further questions?"

Seacord shook his head.

"Very well, then, having digested the above, we'll take a break and go at it again after you have had an opportunity to review your notes."

When they resumed, Bertram had been joined by one of Baxter's specialists from the CSA center, a nondescript little man in an ill-fitting uniform sporting a major's cluster on his collar. When he began to talk, however, what he had to say was more impressive than his appearance.

"I am Major Singleton. Dr. Bertram indicated that you were about to get into the question-and-answer segment of her presentation and invited me to join her. She thought that between the two of us we might be better equipped to answer any questions you may have."

Seacord was ready. He phrased each of his questions carefully. "I have heard rumors that if the Chinese have built a nuclear reactor in the side of a mountain, it may well be an RBMK-1000 design, similar to the Chernobyl 4 unit that failed back in 1986. Any comment on that?"

"You are well informed," Singleton replied. "Although the Russians deny that units such as the reactor that failed at Chernobyl exist outside of Russia, we have reliable information to the contrary. A sale of both technology and support, in addition to materials, did occur. And we have every reason to believe that three more such RBMK-1000 units have since been built elsewhere in China."

Singleton took off his glasses, held them up to the light, and polished them with a handkerchief before he continued. "In our view, the RBMK-1000 reactor design is fatally flawed; each one is an accident waiting to happen. We now know what the Russians learned the hard way April 26, 1986—that the design of the RBMK-1000 requires extensive modification in order to insure reliability. The biggest problem, of course, is that the RBMK-1000 does not use a containment structure. It wasn't until extensive damage and death were attributed to the reactor at Chernobyl that it was determined that such a unit required further containment. The 4 unit at Chernobyl was finally encased in a massive concrete tomb. By then, of course, it was much too late."

Rubbra listened without commenting while Seacord continued to ask questions. "Do we have any real evidence to support the IHO theory that in this situation at Kamanchu we are dealing with a nuclear incident of some type? In other words, Major, could it be something else?"

"We do not have hard evidence," Singleton admitted. "However, when we talk about the Chinese and their nuclear technology, we are dealing with a mixed bag of facts and assumptions. For example, we believe the Chinese possess the technology, the materials, and inclination to build reactors inspired by the RBMK Russian design. As nuclear facilities go, it is inexpensive and easy to construct. But with this particular design, accidents are likely. You ask if it could be something else. Are you suggesting a test gone wrong?" He paused. "It is a possibility. But when we examine the photographs, we are inclined to believe they have had a reactor failure.

"But I hasten to add and admit, there are clearly other possibilities. For example, we cannot rule out the possibility of an accident involving nuclear waste. Either could and would, of course, cause severe damage to the environment and to the populace in that area."

Sheremetyevo Airport
Moscow
4-4

The day prior to their departure for Moscow, Seacord had learned that Hamilton had appointed himself to lead the IHO team. That same Hamilton not only proved to be gregarious and charming during the long flight from Washington to Moscow, he also turned out to be a wealth of knowledge. He had been to Moscow on no less than seven occasions, was fluent in several different languages including Russian, and was well-versed on the effects of radiation on humans and the environment. Seacord used the opportunity to get a better understanding of what Hamilton thought they would be up against when they got to Kamanchu.

Seacord even had the opportunity to ask Hamilton the same question he had asked Singleton. "What do you think we're going to find when we get there?"

Hamilton grimaced and smiled at the same time. "I've wondered the same thing myself. We have to hope that Mother Nature doesn't have something up her sleeve that is even more deadly than a nuclear accident alone. If she does, we're going in cold. We certainly aren't prepared to deal with it. And yet, should that be the case, at least we could come out of it with the satisfaction of knowing we aren't dealing with something as insidious as a pending Chinese attack. I don't think anyone wants to take on the Chinese in a nuclear shoot-out." Hamilton paused before he continued, addressing Seacord by his assumed name. "On the other hand, Dr. Shell, I think that what you are suggesting is highly unlikely. The Swiss are certain there has been some kind of recent nuclear testing in the area. Couple that with a strong indication of radiation contamination, and I would have to agree with Colonel Baxter at the Center for Strategic Assessment. It spells one of two possible likely situations: reactor failure or a nuclear weapons accident of some sort. Apart from that, I don't think it matters much; either way we would have a major problem on our hands."

It was almost an hour later when the Pan Am 747 began its descent into Sheremetyevo. Hamilton had been nodding off, and Seacord was reviewing his notes when the flight attendant began reciting a lengthy list of instructions for deplaning passengers.

By the time the plane had taxied to the terminal, an attractive multilingual flight attendant had regaled them with information on recovering baggage, clearing passport and visa control, customs, obtaining ground transportation into the city, and converting currency.

Seacord, unlike Hamilton, had been in Moscow on only two other occasions; both times before the break up of the Soviet Union. The moment he was inside the terminal, however, he began cataloging the myriad of differences since his last visit. Gone were the blatant banners extolling the virtues of the Party, the legions of sober-faced military guards, and the distinct feeling that, as an American, it would have been better for him not to get off the plane. Sheremetyevo still did not compare with what he was used to back in the States, but the Russian efforts to refurbish and update the sprawling terminal were obvious. It had been painted, sported new furniture, was better lit, and people were more relaxed. Nowhere did he see the hordes of soft-soled KGB men lurking in the shadows.

At the gate of the Pan Am passenger area was a middle-aged man with a puffy face who was wearing a threadbare version of a chauffeur's uniform. He was holding up a crude cardboard sign with the letters IHO printed on it. Underneath, as an obvious afterthought, he had scribbled the word *"Welkome."*

Hamilton headed straight for the man; there was a brief verbal exchange complete with hand gestures, and finally smiles and handshakes. When Hamilton returned, he informed Seacord the man would be waiting for them after they had cleared customs.

Despite the fact that he smiled continuously, the driver of the Chaika limousine had little to say on the drive to the hotel. On one of the few occasions when he did speak, it was to inform them that Chenko had arranged rooms for them at the Belgrade Hotel on Smolensk Street. Each time he spoke, Hamilton had to interpret. "He says Dr. Chenko instructed him to tell us that he and Dr. Chernov will join us for dinner at the Aragvi on Gorky Street at nine o'clock. If we wish, he said he would take us to our hotel, wait for us to check in, then drive us to the restaurant."

Chenko's choice for dinner, the Aragvi, turned out to be one of Moscow's better restaurants. It featured a menu consisting primarily of Georgian cuisine, fare which Hamilton and Seacord quickly learned was

Chenko's favorite. For privacy, the head of the Russian Health Ministry had procured a small private dining room just off the main dining area. Throughout the evening, two elderly waiters seemed both eager and content to stand close by in anticipation of any need.

By the time they had finished a dessert of red berries and cream, Chenko had begun discussing what he called "the new Russia." He talked about the changes since the fall of the Union, and the fact that there were still a great many of his fellow citizens who failed to embrace the new style of government.

"To be critical of our government is a way of life in my country." He sighed. "We Russians would not know what to do if we did not live amidst dissatisfaction and unrest. It is our heritage. As Arkady Sukerov once said, 'If you are not melancholy, you are not Russian.' "

It was only when Chenko finally began to discuss the situation in Kamanchu that Seacord learned Rebi Chernov would be the Russian member of the investigation team. "As always with such matters, there is an unfortunate urgency," Chenko said. "We have only a short time to prepare." Then he revealed something that none of them had been prepared for. "I have taken the liberty of asking a former colleague of mine to meet you at the Mongolian border and serve as your guide. His name is Ugan Sergee. He is a native and he is quite familiar with the Health Ministry in Ulan Bator. Like my friend Dr. Hamilton, Sergee is an old and trusted friend. I have made him aware that the officials in Ulan Bator have rejected our efforts to work with them in investigating the cause of the contamination along the Solonge. Nevertheless, he has agreed to help us. Unofficially, of course; he does not have the sanction of his government."

Hamilton looked unsettled at the news, and Chenko smiled. "I can assure you, Doctor, he knows the area around Kamanchu well. He will be well worth whatever inconvenience you may envision at this change in plans."

Seacord realized Chenko had noticed the uneasy silence that had followed his announcement. Hamilton's face was easy to read. It was obvious Chenko's disclosure had caught him by surprise. Added to that was the fact that Seacord was confident Barrows knew nothing about any additions to the team other than the Russian doctor. As for Chernov, Seacord was unable to tell whether or not she had known about the addition of the Mongolian guide prior to Chenko's announcing the fact.

The dilemma for Seacord was that no one on the IHO team knew anything about the man. Seacord had been trained to anticipate problems, and Ugan Sergee had all the makings of one. Surely Chenko understood they were going into what could well turn out to be a dicey situation. The obvious questions were, could this Sergee be trusted, and would he be able to pull his weight if the going got tough? The way Seacord saw it, he was already saddled with protecting two doctors. Was the Mongolian guide going to be any better?

That question was still unanswered when Rebi Chernov caught the mood at the table and lifted her glass in a toast. "It is the custom in my country to drink to our past and our heritage, but tonight I think it more appropriate that we drink to the spirit of co-operation. To you, Dr. Shell and Dr. Hamilton, both Dr. Chenko and I say thank you. Without your efforts, Dr. Hamilton, I have no doubt that this effort would not have materialized."

Seacord lifted his glass of vodka in unison with the others. As he did, it occurred to him that he would have enjoyed Rebi Chernov's toast even more if it had been a brand of familiar scotch or even a good cold American beer.

"And with that," Chenko concluded, "I suggest we retire to savor our dinner, get a good night's rest, and be about the business of your visit first thing tomorrow morning. I will have the driver take you back to your hotel when you are ready. I will have him call for you at eight o'clock tomorrow morning. We have much to accomplish and not a great deal of time in which to accomplish it."

Seacord looked at Hamilton. He had heard the same words from Barrows some seventy-two hours earlier, and although he didn't say as much, he was beginning to feel the same sense of urgency.

Back in his room at the Belgrade, Seacord showered and reflected back over what had been a long day. Duplicating what Hamilton had done for their hosts, Chenko had provided the Americans with the Russian version of dossiers on the two members of the team with whom they would be working. There was an in-depth bio on Rebi Chernov, and a lesser one on Ugan Sergee. In Chernov's bio, Chenko had focused on her work in the GRU prior to joining the Health Ministry. Seacord reasoned that if she really was a graduate of the GRU Academy as the bio indicated, he could quit worrying. She could handle more than he had originally given her credit for.

When he finished, Seacord turned back to the cover page on Chernov's dosier and read it a second time.

Name: Rebi Katrina Chernov
Birth date: 05/05/67
Height: 5' 8"
Married: XXXX
Birthplace: Odessa
Education: University of Odessa-ITNA
Rostov-Collegium-ADD
GRU Academy (classified)

A note at the bottom of the page read:

Dr. Chernov is a respected biophysicist who has been with Slovadoka Pokavast for the past nine years. Her specialty is biomedicine and forensic studies. Also noteworthy is her special training: graduate of the GRE Academy.

When Seacord finished reading the bio, he laid the document on the bed. Chernov hadn't said much at dinner earlier that evening, but on paper she appeared to be more than capable. Completing GRU training spoke volumes.

The Sergee folder contained far less information. Chenko indicated that Sergee, like Chernov, had also been a GRU agent. Other than that, there wasn't a lot to go on. Either Chenko hadn't had much contact with Sergee in recent years, or there wasn't that much to tell. The bottom line on Sergee's file, however, was there was simply not enough information in it to make Seacord feel confident.

On the plus side was the fact that both Sergee and the woman had passed through the GRE academy, indicating that at one time at least, they had both received extensive special training and were combat-skilled. He remembered what Barrows had once said about anyone who had made it through training at the Spetsnaz. "It's been my experience that they are pretty much like jungle cats; they have learned how to kill their adversary—and in most cases they are able to achieve their objective before the unfortunate victim is even able to detect their presence."

Seacord closed the file and laid it back on the bed. If Barrows was right, he thought, he would have second thoughts about asking Rebi Chernov for a date.

Zijin Mountain Project
Kamanchu
4-5

It was late. PRK Captain Xin Tsu Lea had completed his last round of the day and retired to his temporary quarters for the night. The site was high on a hill next to one of the two access roads leading to a vantage point overlooking the entrance to the Zijin Mountain facility. From where he stood he could see little of the actual base. The distant lights merely indicated the location of the security perimeter.

As he pulled his chair up to the small table he used for a desk and turned on the lamp, he began mentally composing the wording of the day's entry in his journal. In the background he could hear both the weather and the reassuring sound of the small generator that provided power.

It had been nearly a month since the collapse of the bridge and the wreck of the train destined for Ulan Bator. Base officials had not discovered the wreckage for two whole days, and only then because rail authorities in Ulan Bator had informed Colonel Kang that the train had not arrived on schedule.

That same day a detail had been dispatched, the wreckage discovered, and the extent of the damage determined. It was the description of the ravaged countryside by one of Kang's young officers that had caused Kang to contact Beijing and ask for assistance in cleaning up. In that same report, Kang, in addition to describing the magnitude of the problem, had also detailed the sudden deadly epidemic that had hit the Zijin Mountain operation.

It had taken three days for Kang to receive a response from his superiors in Beijing. When it came, the orders stunned him. Instead of informing him that they were sending the anticipated assistance, Kang was ordered to secure the area around the base, post guards, and make certain no one entered or left the site. The fate of the personnel Kang believed to be trapped inside the mountain was not addressed.

Because Xin was first and foremost a loyal officer of the PRK, he had followed his commander's orders to the letter. Like Kang, he waited, only to learn that Beijing's initial response was followed for the next several days with communiques detailing the precautions that should betaken. Nothing was said about sending help. As Xin sat at his makeshift desk, listening to sleet pepper the roof of the small building, he was worried. He was keenly aware that it had been over a week since he had received any word from either his commander or Beijing. His daily communiques as well as his repeated requests for medical assistance and supplies went unacknowledged. He had even begun to wonder if Kang and the other members of his staff had succumbed to the illness that had befallen many of his own men.

Finally Xin opened his journal, penned the date, and began to write:

> Twice within the past week I have assigned a small detail of men to review the situation outside the entrance to the mountain. They continue to report that there is no evidence of activity in or around areas accessible to the base. It has now been seven days since we have been able to establish contact with anyone to determine whether or not there are any still alive inside the complex itself.
>
> I have repeatedly attempted to establish communication with the base, but have been unable to do so.

Xin stopped for several minutes before continuing. He was chilled. The weather in the past few days had been steadily deteriorating. There had been heavy rains during the daylight hours that frequently changed to sleet and sometimes snow at night. That weather, coupled with the occasional earth tremors and the lack of response from his superiors, made it difficult for him to go about his duties.

Finally he rose, walked to the corner of the room, and stood by the small heater to ward off the chill. Then he went back to his desk, picked up his pen, and began to write again.

> I continue to file my reports in the hope that someone at headquarters is receiving them.
>
> My assumption continues to be that at least some of the technicians were able to make it to protected areas, but even if they did, there is no way to get food, water, or other supplies to them.
>
> Equally disturbing, in addition to the concern for the health of the men under my command, is an awareness that the material in the weapons assembly area may no longer be properly attended. If that is the case, the plutonium could become unstable and the situation worsen.

Then he added the words that he could not bring himself to author in his previous entries.

> I now fear that all five hundred and thirty-one people inside the Zijin facility are near death or have already died.

At that point Xin quit writing. He was exhausted. His mind, as it had so frequently over the past several days, began to stray, and he found it difficult to concentrate. To ward off sleep, he pushed himself away from the table, stood up, and walked to the room's only window. Even with the heavy combination of rain and sleet, he could see that the security lights around the entrance to the complex were still burning. He walked back to his bunk, sat down, and experienced the futile loneliness of the moment.

Saint Francis Hospital
Washington
4-6

At twenty-four years of age, Shelly Martin had more problems than she could deal with. In addition to a cocaine habit and mounting debts, her situation had worsened when she recently discovered she was pregnant.

Single, and a recent graduate of a nursing program at a nearby night school, Shelly had had good prospects for the future until she met Antonio Gibbs. Instead, that day had turned out to be the beginning of a nightmare—a situation that for Shelly Martin had become a living hell. After learning she was pregnant, Gibbs had moved out, leaving her with a mountain of debt. Shelly hadn't heard from Antonio in six weeks when he finally called. That call only served to make everything worse.

He had asked her to meet him at a local bar after she got off work. Thinking a reconciliation might be in the offing, she agreed to meet him.

When she met Gibbs, to Shelly's surprise, he wasn't alone. Gibbs's friend turned out to be a pale, awkward-looking man wearing a baseball cap and a leather jacket. But other then the small mole on his cheek and the fact that he had a curious way of talking, there was little else she could remember about the man.

Gibbs, on the other hand, treated the man he introduced as Richie Beard like an old friend. "Tony tells me you work at Saint Francis Hospital," Beard began. "He says you're a nurse."

Shelly nodded. When she thought about it, earning her degree, passing her boards, and receiving an offer of employment from the small hospital were about the only things in her life she could be proud of.

"He also tells me you work sometimes in the IC unit," Beard continued.

"Most of the time," she clarified. "But sometimes, when things are slow, I'm told to go down and work in pediatrics. Why?"

Instead of answering her question, Beard reached in his pocket and removed a small envelope. He opened it and laid five crisp new one-hundred-dollar bills on the table in front of her. "I'll bet you don't know what I do for a livin', sugar," he said. Then he added, "Of course you don't. You just met me, right?"

Shelly Martin would have readily acknowledged she was not very good at judging people. Antonio Gibbs was proof of that. But about Richie Beard she had already come to one conclusion; the man was enchanted with the sound of his own voice.

"Well, sugar, I'm one of those guy's that's got a real interestin' job. I'm an arranger. Which means I *arrange* things. I make things happen. Follow?"

Shelly wasn't at all sure she knew how Antonio's friend expected her to respond. It had taken her less than ten minutes to decide she disliked him, but she couldn't take her eyes off of the money. "What kind of things?" she finally asked.

Beard glanced at Gibbs. "You got a bright girl here,

Tony boy. She knows what kind of questions to ask." Then he looked back at Shelly again. "Ever read them supermarket rags? You know, the ones you see when you're standin' in the checkout lane."

"I've seen them, but I don't read them."

"Hey, no sweat, sugar. Beardsy here doesn't care what you read as long as you know what I'm talkin' about, right?"

"I guess," Shelly admitted. Then she looked at her former boyfriend. "What's this all about, Tony?"

Before Tony could answer, Beard cut in. "I got me a friend, Sugar. This friend, he works for one of them rags I was tellin' you about. He makes good money. And he's on to somethin'. He thinks there's a story in that guy you got in your IC unit over at the hospital."

"You mean the man that was beat up in the parking lot of that bar?" Shelly asked.

"You're alive, Sugar, I mean really alive. That's the one I'm talkin' about."

"I've never actually seen him," Shelly admitted.

"Ever since he's been there, there has been a policeman just outside the IC unit. I wouldn't be able to get this friend of yours in if that's what you want."

"That's not what I'm askin', Sugar." Beard took time to light a cigarette and admire the cloud of slate-colored smoke as he exhaled. "What I want, sugar, ain't really all that complicated. All I want you to do is get me a couple of pictures of that guy. You know, snapshots. That's all. Easy, huh?"

Shelly continued to stare at the money. "Pictures,

that's all? Nothin' kinky? Just pictures? Nothing else?"

Beard reached in his jacket pocket again, and this time his hand emerged with a small 35mm camera. It was the smallest camera Shelly had ever seen. "Just a couple of snapshots, Sugar. The camera is already loaded—infrared film so you don't need no flash. All you gotta to do is aim it, press this little button, take the pictures, walk out of the room, call me, and I'll stop by and pick up the camera. In return for a few minutes of your time, I hand over these nice new pictures of Ben Franklin. Not bad for a couple of minutes work, huh? I'll bet you don't make that much workin' for the hospital in a week, right?"

Shelly Martin needed money, and because of that she agreed to Beard's proposal. Two days later she found herself standing at the third-floor nurses' station with a tray containing the midnight meds for the patients in the IC unit. She had studied the chart. She knew the configuration of the beds in the IC unit. And she knew that the patient Tony's friend wanted pictures of was at the far end of the unit. The patient's bed was separated from the other beds by nothing more than a screen and the presence of the private-duty nurse assigned to monitor his progress.

In addition to knowing the layout of the room, Shelly had learned the name of the private-duty nurse on the midnight shift and that the IC unit supervisor was Arlene Ingram. And she had used the previous night's med charts to determine the kind of medicines she was expected to pass.

The officer at the door to the IC unit was seated at a small card table, idly paging through a copy of *Playboy*. He looked up when Shelly approached. "Where's Margaret?" he asked. "She usually brings me a cup of coffee when she passes the midnight meds."

Shelly raised her eyebrow and managed to put together a smile. She was doing everything she could to keep her voice from shaking. "Hey," she was finally able to get out. "I didn't know I was supposed to play stewardess to you guys, too. I'll get you some as soon as I pass meds, okay?"

The officer glanced at the tray, sighed, stood up, and opened the door for her. Getting past him had been far less difficult then she had anticipated. She had expected to be nervous, maybe even shake when she talked to the officer, but she was inside now and looking at the IC unit charge nurse, Arlene Ingram.

"Here are the midnight meds, but before I forget, I'm supposed to tell you that you have a telephone call at the nurses' station," she said. "If you want to take it, I'll watch things until you get back; providing you don't take too long. I was suppose to get off duty fifteen minutes ago."

Shelly breathed a sigh of relief when Arlene did not question her. Instead, the woman complained briefly that the call could have been transferred if anyone would have thought to do so. She vacillated momentarily before she said, "Watch the light on 5C; his nurse went down to the cafeteria to grab a sandwich. I'm supposed to be watching him."

"What do I do if—"

"Don't worry, he probably won't give you any trouble; he hasn't made a sound all evening."

Shelly Martin waited until she heard the door close. Then she set the tray down, walked to the far end of the unit, pulled back the screen, took out the camera, and aimed. If infrared film worked like Tony's friend said it did, she had just made five hundred dollars and her life was definitely on the upswing. Just like that, she had more than enough money for the abortion.

It was almost dawn by the time Richie Beard was able to get one of his friends to develop the film. What he saw amazed him, and he hurried to the phone and made the call. "Nikko," he began, his voice sounding even raspier than usual. "I need to talk to Chen."

The voice on the other end of the line was a thick half-growl. "For Christ sake, Beardsy, you got any idea what time it is? It ain't even six o'clock yet. He's still asleep."

"Wake him up. I got something important to tell him."

"Tell me. I'll relay the message when he wakes up."

Richie Beard, a little man who had spent most of his life hanging on to the frayed edges of his seamy world, was momentarily tempted to tell his contact he would call back when he knew Chen Ton was awake. This was his chance—a chance to score—a chance to become more important to Chen.

But he was too impatient; like so many times before, Richie Beardsy forfeited his opportunity. Instead of waiting, he blurted out the reason for his call. "Tell the man I got pictures."

"Pictures of what?" Nikko grunted.

"Of the guy they got in the IC unit over at Saint Francis. Tell Mr. Chen he was right. It's a goddamn setup. There ain't nothin' in that bed but a fuckin' dummy."

Chapter Five

Kolomenskoye Estate
31 Proletarsky Prospekt
Moscow
5-1

As far as Seacord was concerned, the director of the Russian Health Ministry had selected a curious site for the first briefing of the IHO team. Seacord had pictured something slightly clandestine. But that wasn't the word for the place where Chenko had taken them; inspiring, he decided, would have been more fitting.

From where Seacord was sitting he could see the famous sixteenth-century Church of the Ascension of Christ, a tent-shaped stone structure that Rebi Chernov proudly informed him was the first of its kind built in Russia. Even the room where Chenko had assembled them looked and felt like a museum. Everywhere Seacord looked there were examples of the opulence that had been decried by the Party during their long reign over the Russian people. The Kolomenskoye estate was itself a maze of rotundas and pavilions. Everywhere he looked there were examples of Russian porcelains, antique ceramics, pottery, and glass. It occurred to him that Kat would have appreciated the ambience of the old building a great deal more than he ever would.

Chenko had started the meeting promptly at eight-thirty, marshaling them around an ornate black walnut table trimmed with gold inlay. The walls of the room were covered with tapestries and seventeenth-century paintings. Despite the formality of the setting, the unexpected accoutrements of coffee and rolls were also present. "For our American friends," Chenko crowed, holding up a can of American coffee. "Perhaps someday we Russians will also acquire a taste for this mild curiosity as well."

If Josef Chenko seemed slightly ebullient, Rebi Chernov was his antithesis. She was, unlike the night before, sober-faced and decidedly less gregarious than her mentor. When Chenko finished his opening remarks, he called upon her. She began by unrolling a composite chart of the area where the IHO team would be conducting its investigation. As she discussed each of the features on the larger map, she produced smaller, more detailed diagrams to highlight the areas that required emphasis.

"We will start with the Jingsan Dam," she said. "You will notice that it is located approximately seven kilometers south and east of the village of Kamanchu. According to our intelligence people, the population of the village is less than one thousand at this time of year. The vast majority of them are employed either at the dam site or in the Zijin facility itself. Those that aren't involved with the activities inside the complex are mostly children.

"Construction of the Jingsan Dam began some five years prior to any noticeable building activity near the Kamanchu site at the base of Zijin Mountain. Perhaps I should also mention that until work on the dam began, this area of Mongolia, which is both mountainous and quite heavily forested, was virtually without inhabitants. Except, of course, for the few sparsely populated villages you see indicated on the maps. All of this construction, of course, occurred during that period when the Chinese occupied Mongolia."

Seacord interrupted. "Dr. Chernov, I'm curious. Is there some reason why your government did not investigate the thinking behind the Chinese building this facility so close to the border? Among other oddities, it appears to be in an area where there would be no real need for a dam of that size."

"The world as we knew it was quite different then, Dr. Shell. Despite centuries of border disputes and mistrust that have historically been the nature of our relationship with the Chinese, at the time they were our allies. When the Jingsan Dam was being constructed, we shared similar ideologies. Our biggest concern in those days, if you will forgive me, was the capitalist war machine of the United States. Our view of the Jingsan Dam project at that time was that the PRC was simply manifesting the doctrines of Chairman Mao and Lenin; that is to say, improving the lives of the people."

When Chernov finished she looked around the room as though she were anticipating a rebuttal from either Hamilton or Seacord. "You must understand that it is the way things were then"—she shrugged—"not the way they are now."

Chenko smiled. It was obvious he was pleased with the manner in which his protégé had fielded Seacord's question. There was no call for apologies and she had offered none; history was history. "Please proceed, Dr. Chernov," he urged.

"The dam itself is approximately two hundred meters high, and nearly four hundred and eighty meters long. If you are looking for something to compare it to, I am told it approximates what you once referred to as your Teton Dam. Our engineers estimate that it is at least two hundred and fifty meters thick, and contains slightly more than three million cubic meters of backfill.

"During the last twelve months our analysts report seeing some evidence of erosion at the site, and they have even gone so far as to predict that the structure may well eventually become unstable. As one analyst at Kirensk has pointed out, we have seen no evidence that the Chinese are making any attempt at maintenance. Perhaps that is because, as Dr. Shell points out, there is very little real need for the dam.

"The waters of two rivers, the Menges and the Kantapol, feed into the reservoir, and when the water is released it forms the Solonge. The Solonge, of course, pools at that point, downstream from the village of Kamanchu, and flows to the northeast where the pollution was first detected.

"We have no official figures, of course, because the Chinese, as is their custom, continue to be evasive about the dam's purpose. Our engineers estimate, however, that if the Chinese chose to use it as a power source, the Jingsan Dam should be capable of producing at least one million kilowatts—perhaps more."

Seacord noticed that up to that point, the effusive Hamilton had been somewhat reticent. Now, however, he was leaning forward, studying the map, and comparing it to the Chernov diagrams. "I'm interested in your response to Dr. Shell's question; why would they build such a facility when there are so few people in the area and no apparent need for all that power?"

"That question surfaces now, but we did not wonder at the outset," Chernov said. "The reason for the dam became somewhat more obvious when the Chinese began construction of a facility at the base of Zijin Mountain. That construction, of course, began several years later." The woman again pointed to her map, this time to an area north-northwest of the dam site. "At the time there was a great deal of surface construction that was readily visible, and work appeared to be progressing until earthquakes struck the area in the early nineties. Again I believe that it is worth mentioning that the PRC made no attempt to conceal what they were doing."

"And you say that after the series of earthquakes

they began to dismantle the facility?" Seacord was doing his best to understand the time line.

"That is correct, Dr. Shell," Chernov agreed. Then she smiled and looked around the room. "I must be careful how I word this. I trust that none of our esteemed generals are lurking in the shadows, Dr. Chenko?"

The director shook his head and returned her smile.

"Then I feel at liberty to say that this is where, as you Americans say, 'we dropped the ball.' Because we believed they were dismantling the facility at Kamanchu, we failed to give it the proper attention. That continued to be the case until the railroad was completed some four years ago. Only then did we again become aware of the increased activity in terms of both the number of personnel traveling to and from Ulan Bator and in the amount of materials and supplies being shipped to Kamanchu."

Hamilton looked at Chenko. "Is it safe for us to assume, Josef, that you and your people have verified and confirmed all of Dr. Chernov's suspicions?"

Chenko smiled at his old friend. "We have been able to verify all of the information we are presenting," he said. "As you well know, we are a cautious and, at times, a suspicious people. I can assure you that we are not relying on Dr. Chernov's observations and concerns alone. Suffice to say, we have verified what it is possible to verify. There are times when our prior assumptions prove valuable and times when they mean nothing. . . ."

"What kind of weather will we encounter?" Seacord asked.

Chernov was prepared. She passed out a packet entitled *Climatological Assessment.* "In a word, Dr. Shell, we can expect the weather to be quite unpleasant. I have had conversations with our climatologists and meteorologists. They point out that while it is not officially winter in Kamanchu, it will be quite cold and quite windy. I am told we can expect excessive precipitation in the form of rain, and occasionally sleet and snow. The terrain in that part of Mongolia at this time of year is not unlike the weather you would expect in the foothills of your Western states. There is one concern, however, that should not be dismissed lightly. We must also be alert to the possibility of further seismic activity. We know that there have been a series of cluster quakes in the region recently, and the Swiss reported a 7.2 earthquake near Kamanchu less than a month ago."

"It doesn't exactly sound like a Caribbean vacation," Seacord quipped.

Chernov smiled. Barrows was right. She was one good-looking filly.

"I haven't even mentioned the 'cold rain' yet," she said.

"Cold rain?" Seacord repeated.

"In Russia we call it cold rain. You Americans call it dirty rain. Different countries call it different things."

"What Dr. Chernov is talking about is any form of precipitation that has the potential for carrying radioactive pollutants," Hamilton clarified. "The conditions for cold rain would appear to be abundant in an area such as Kamanchu."

Chernov nodded agreement. "It is as Dr. Hamilton says. There is a high probability we will encounter it in some form, and we must be prepared for that."

"Based on what I've heard here this morning, it appears as though you and Dr. Chenko have a pretty good idea what we'll be up against when we get there," Seacord said. "But the one we haven't addressed comes when we have to find a way past the PRK border guards."

"That is where Ugan Sergee comes in," Chenko said.

"Which brings me to my next question," Seacord continued. "We appreciate the extensive dossier on Dr. Chernov. But the background information on your friend Ugan Sergee is rather sketchy. I'm sure Dr. Hamilton and I, as well as Dr. Chernov, would appreciate knowing a little more about the man."

For the briefest of moments it seemed like Chenko was hedging. "I first became aware of Ugan Sergee when he was an illegal with the GRU. He was stationed in Ulan Bator at the time, and my colleagues in both the GRU and the KGB used his services extensively up until the mid-seventies. The information he was able to provide us was invaluable. Since then I have maintained contact, admittedly limited, with him. Consequently, when Dr. Chernov first voiced her concerns about the situation at Kamanchu, I contacted him to find out what he knew. He informed me he was aware that there had been at least two and possibly three different rail shipments of nuclear waste from Kamanchu. All of them, he claimed, were destined for disposal at an undisclosed site in the Gobi."

"Was he aware or did he say anything about a reactor malfunction at Kamanchu?" Seacord questioned.

Chenko shook his head. "I addressed that very matter. He indicated he had heard nothing of a malfunction, but he also said he would be willing to ask a few questions. Three days later he reported back to me that he was unable to verify that there had been an accident or that there even was a reactor. By then I knew of Dr. Hamilton's plan to put together a team to investigate the situation, and I inquired about Sergee's availability to serve as a guide."

"Bottom line, you're telling us you trust him with no reservations," Seacord pressed. "Is that right?"

"And you're convinced that he knows the territory?" Hamilton added.

"As well as anyone knows the territory in and around Kamanchu," Chenko said. "Outside of the Jingsan Dam, the Chinese installation at Kamanchu, and the fact that such an area even exists, there really isn't that much to know."

Hamilton closed his folder. The tone of his voice revealed his impatience. "So when do we go?"

"Your flight leaves for Irkutsk tomorrow at noon. It is a long one—seven hours, I believe," Chenko said. "Most of everything you will require has been shipped ahead: supplies, gear, equipment. However, it will be necessary for Dr. Chernov to check out the equipment and make certain everything is in working order when you get there."

"What about the equipment we brought with us?" Seacord asked.

"I have taken the liberty of having it sent on to Irkutsk instead of having it go through customs here in Moscow," Chenko said. "It will be waiting for you—as will Mr. Sergee."

Ulan Bator
Mongolian People's Republic
Hotel Bayangol
5-2

Ugan Sergee, it was said, was a man motivated by money. The son of a former career diplomat and a Russian mother, he had been educated in schools in Switzerland and Russia, and recruited by the GRU shortly after finishing his formal education. After that he was sent to the Soviet Academy at Frunze, where he was trained for his role in the GRU.

As a GRU illegal in his native land, he enjoyed instant success. His familiarity with the way things worked in the Mongolian capital enabled him to contribute from the outset. Because of his father's numerous political connections, few doors were closed to him. He spoke both Chinese and Russian, and was comfortably familiar with a number of Mongolian regional dialects.

Now forty-six years old, he was no longer an agent. He carried the card of a low-level official in the Ulan Bator government, but lived by his wits. Ugan Sergee sold skills, knowledge, loyalties, information, or secrets to the country or individual who would pay him the most money.

Despite his somewhat oafish appearance and demeanor, Ugan Sergee was very good at reading the faces, judging the attire, and assessing the body language of anyone he encountered. He liked to boast that he could read most people well enough to determine their profession, their interests, and their concerns. It was a skill that served him well. As a former GRU illegal, his efficiency, and on occasion even his life, had depended on that skill.

Now, as he sat in the hotel dining room waiting for Mishbib to get down to business, he amused himself by scrutinizing others in the busy room. It was a game. The woman at the table to his left was doubtless Korean, and probably involved in some fashion with the current trade mission that had been visiting his city for the past two days. It was equally obvious she had not acquired a taste for the *buudz,* the small steamed pastry she had ordered for her lunch.

To his immediate right were two Chinese PRK officers, both young and animated. Sergee could not help but wonder if they were stationed at the very installation his old acquaintance, Josef Chenko, had been speaking of in their phone conversations over the past two weeks.

Ugan Sergee was not a tall man, at five-eight in height and weighing close to 240 pounds, his physical uniqueness evolved out of his robust appearance. He was barrel-chested, bald, mustached, and possessed penetrating black eyes that shifted impatiently during the course of his conversations.

Thirty minutes after sitting down with his old friend, he finished his *arkhi,* but found himself still waiting for Mishbib Antan to finally get around to the point.

Mishbib, like Sergee, had no official title. But it was generally accepted that he would be the one who represented the PRK or PRC when it came to discussing delicate matters with officials in the Ulan Bator government. Over the past several years Mishbib and Sergee had met and conducted business on numerous occasions.

"Now that you have had your fill," Sergee finally said, "suppose we discuss the reason for this meeting. After all, my friend, you are the one who contacted me."

Mishbib had not quite finished his bowl of *hoitzer,* but he shoved the remainder of the large bowl of mutton stew to the middle of the table and lit a cigarette. "There is a situation," Mishbib began, "of which my comrades and I are convinced you are already aware. We are told that the Russians have requested permission from your government to investigate what they believe to be a health hazard. Is that so?" The man wheezed as he spoke.

Sergee took another sip of his *arkhi* and played with the half-empty glass, rolling it back and forth between the palms of his oversized hands. "And what exactly is this health hazard you think I am aware of?" he asked.

Mishbib liked to play with words. "Did I say there actually was a health hazard?"

Sergee smiled. He was willing to wait. Time was on his side. He knew that eventually the fat man would have to get around to what was on his mind.

"It really does not matter so much whether there is or is not a health hazard in so remote an area of our republic," Mishbib continued. "That is not the issue. The issue is, it would be most unfortunate if an expedition by unauthorized representatives of the International Health Organization was permitted to go into the area in question and look around."

"Unfortunate for who?" Sergee taunted.

Mishbib dismissed the question and reached for his stew again.

"Do not delude yourself." Sergee smiled. "If your comrades are concerned that this team of investigators will discover what they have attempted to conceal in Zijin Mountain, you should tell them its existence is already common knowledge. Even I know what the PRK is doing there. If I know it, it is not a well-kept secret."

"Zijin Mountain?" Mishbib repeated blankly.

Sergee shook his head and ordered another *arkhi*. "You disappoint me, Mishbib. I am the one who frequently plays the role of a fool to my advantage. You are not good at it, and you are being less then honest with me. If I am wrong, suppose you tell me what your Chinese friends are really concerned about."

Mishbib hesitated. "What I am about to tell you must be held in the strictest confidence. You must repeat it to no one. Is that understood?"

Sergee continued to smile, and in the process revealed several gold teeth and the voids between them. "Come, come. You knew you could trust me or you would not have come to me."

Mishbib had lost the duel of words, and the expression on his usually fatuous face exposed the fact that he was uneasy with the prospect of telling Sergee more than he had been authorized to reveal. "The PRK and consequently some PRC leaders are aware that the Russians and perhaps others know they have built a nuclear facility in the side of a mountain near Kamanchu. It is difficult to conceal such matters from the prying eyes of satellites. But my friends in Kamanchu and Beijing are equally convinced that there is a great deal more about this facility that the Russians and Americans do not know."

"Such as?"

"That is not for me to reveal. It is enough for me to say that it serves our best interests not to have outsiders snooping into the nature of our activity in Kamanchu."

Sergee leaned back in his chair and laughed. "You are being evasive, my friend, and you are not very good at it."

Mishbib cleared his throat. "Unfortunately, within the past few weeks, there has been an accident—a very minor accident, but nevertheless an accident. Apparently that accident has been brought to the attention of and alarmed some in the international community."

"Minor accident?" Sergee laughed. "Come, come. It is rumored there was a meltdown," Sergee challenged.

"Nothing so dramatic, comrade. There was not a meltdown." Mishbib was emphatic. "I can assure you, there was not a meltdown because there is a no longer any such thing as a reactor at Kamanchu. That was a dream that was dispensed with years ago when we realized how unstable the earth was." He paused, then finally added, "I have already told you all that I can tell you, perhaps even more than I should. But we are friends, no? Friends trust friends."

"We are business associates," Sergee corrected.

"My purpose in coming here is to inquire what you know about the Russian response to this situation. We know you have been contacted."

"My curiosity is raised, old man." Sergee continued to grin. "How do you know I have been contacted?"

It was Mishbib's turn to enjoy the moment. He leaned forward and lowered his voice. "Ahhh, we live in a world of subterfuge and espionage, my careless friend. You have grown derelict as you have grown fat around the middle. Your GRU instructors would be disappointed. Your calls are routed through the switchboard of your apartment house, are they not? When you began receiving calls from the Ministry of Health in Moscow, we were informed. It is a simple matter to monitor telephone calls. We are quite aware that you have been hired to guide a team of IHO officials to the site of our recent misfortune at Kamanchu. And that is precisely what our friends in the PRK do not want to happen."

Sergee studied what remained of his drink. Mishbib was right. He had not been overly careful, and he knew exactly what the man was driving at. "Tell me, my friend. Just how badly do they want to avoid having this mysterious whatever discovered?"

Mishbib Antan took off his glasses and made a pretense of cleaning them. "I am authorized to see that you are paid a very handsome sum if you will see to it that the IHO team does not discover our little secret."

Finally, the clowning and verbal sparring was over. The mention of money had elevated the conversation to what Sergee liked to think was serious. Sergee resorted to a frown, and began drumming his fingers on the table. "Tell me, Mishbib, why don't your Chinese comrades take the simple precaution of doubling their guards at this supposedly secret facility?

It should be a simple matter of dispatching a few extra men to—"

Mishbib's round, usually bland face was flushed. "That is being done. But it cannot be done in time to insure . . ."

Sergee waved his hand. "Never mind. How much?"

"As you well know, my Chinese friends can be quite generous. It has been suggested that perhaps the IHO team could meet with an unfortunate accident."

"Accidents cost even more money than getting conveniently lost. I repeat. How much?"

Mishbib Antan took out a pen, scribbled a number on a piece of paper, and handed it to Sergee.

Sergee was surprised. The PRC offer was generous. Enough so that he did not feel he had to negotiate. "The offer is agreeable, but I will need the sum in advance. It is not you I distrust, my friend; it is your associates." Sergee waited for the terms of his demand to sink in. He was holding all the cards, and he was confident his friend realized it. "You can tell your comrades I am quite capable of addressing their needs. But only if you meet me here tonight with the money. By this time tomorrow I will already be on my way to Irkutsk."

"It will be difficult for me to obtain your fee by tonight," Mishbib complained. "Arrangements have to be made".

Sergee smiled. "Now it is you who are playing games with me, my friend. If your comrades would like me to arrange an accident, I feel certain you will find a way."

Vilnius, 12 Butlerova
Moscow
5-3

The Vilnius on Butlerova enjoyed a reputation as one of Moscow's finer restaurants. It served primarily Lithuanian fare, and the setting presented the IHO team with a better opportunity to get to know each other.

Following dinner, though, Chenko again referred to his health and asked to be excused. "At my age I consider myself fortunate just to make it through the day. The maladies of age and the tribulations of infirmities make it imperative that I retire earlier than in days past. Will you forgive me?"

Shortly afterward, Hamilton embraced the same routine. Like Chenko, he confessed to not "feeling up to par." He had managed to stay through most of the evening, but offered his apologies after the meal's final course. His departure left Seacord and Rebi Chernov at the table alone.

"I take it that you have not been to Moscow for some time?" Rebi began.

"It's been a while," Seacord admitted. "I see a big change."

Chernov, in addition to being attractive, was gracious. "I will take that as a compliment. However, the reviews are still coming in. Some like the changes. Others do not. The Communists continue to agitate. I'm afraid they still make a great deal of noise at times when silence would be better served."

"Old ways die hard," Seacord said with a sigh. The moment he said it, he knew there was a ring of trite finality to what he had said. Not exactly the way to keep a conversation going. Kat was right. After all these years he still had a long way to go to be an engaging conversationalist. He tried to recover by adding, "These past several years must have been a trying time for you."

Chernov tilted her head to one side. "Is a noncommittal posture on social change required of all G7 agents?" she asked. The question was unexpected and uncompromising. Seacord disliked being caught off guard. He knew Barrows would have said he should have seen it coming.

He waited several moments before he answered. "Would it do me any good to say something like I don't know what you are talking about?"

"It would be pointless. Men are never good liars."

"So—how did you know?"

At that particular moment, Rebi Chernov looked more like a mischievous schoolgirl than a former GRU operative. There was a blush of color in her cheeks that hadn't been apparent earlier. Behind her, a trio of strolling violinists were playing a song that to Seacord sounded like it came from the soundtrack of an old Ingrid Bergman movie.

"I am a voracious reader, Dr. Shell, or is it all right to call you Agent Seacord now? T. J. Seacord, isn't it? I speak five different languages, and your American weekly newsmagazines intrigue me. Why? Because your American journalists often seem at odds with the stance of your government. That is seldom the way in my country. Editorials criticizing the government here are rarely voiced unless they appear in one of our underground publications. You were quite correct when you observed that old ways die hard."

Seacord saw no need to reply. Rebi Chernov was not only refreshing, she was exceedingly clever. She had the opportunity, but refused to launch into the old philosophical diatribes of the Party.

"As for how I knew, that part is easy to explain," she went on. "I saw your picture in an article I was reading about what your journalists call the 'Bridgewater affair' in your country. Does that satisfy your curiosity?"

"I have to ask, does Chenko know?"

The Russian shook her head. Even in the harsh lighting of the Vilnius dining room, the gesture was arrantly feminine. Seacord was keeping score: bright, articulate, attractive, well-read, inquisitive. What else? The doctor was turning out to be nothing at all like T. J. had anticipated. "No, Dr. Chenko does not know," she admitted. "And until a few moments ago even I could not be certain. If you had denied it, I might have doubted you, but I would have had no way of validating my suspicions."

"So what happens now? Do you blow the whistle and send me home with my government tail between my legs?"

"It does not work that way. On the contrary, now it is your turn. You can satisfy my somewhat morbid curiosity by answering a couple of my questions."

"Like what?"

"One would have to be blind not to notice the remnants of the cuts and bruises on your face. In addition, on several occasions I have noticed a slight limp. Naturally this raises the question of whether or not you are physically up to our little excursion into Kamanchu."

Seacord was amused. "I think I can handle it. Can you?"

Rebi started to laugh. "Ahhh, a challenge. I like challenges. But you are evading my questions. Nevertheless, I will answer yours. I am not a schoolgirl, Agent Seacord. I feel reasonably certain your government has a good reason for this little charade. You can rest assured I will tell no one if whatever logic brings you to Moscow does not interfere with the purpose of our investigation."

Unless Hamilton and his IHO team were willing to go all the way back to square one, Seacord knew he had no choice but to take the woman at her word. He decided to explain. "The way my government sees it, Dr. Hamilton is marching into uncharted territory. There are any number of people back home that believe the IHO is in over their collective head on this one. So, they sent me along. The main reason I'm here is to see that Hamilton doesn't get bushwhacked."

Rebi Chernov repeated the word. "Bushwhacked? What a curious term—what does this word mean?"

"It means I'm here to protect Hamilton's flank, his back, and any other exposed body parts. Miles Hamilton is a medical man first and an investigator second. We don't know what he's capable of handling, and it's my job to make certain he doesn't back himself into a corner or get himself shot."

"And that is your only purpose in being here?"

"Look, Dr. Chernov, this isn't a case of just another

American agency poking its nose into someone else's business. We happen to believe there is a great deal at stake here, and our concern is more than just the pollution. We have had reports of underground nuclear tests in the area. Added to that is the fact that for some time now my country has been investigating the theft of nuclear technology by the Chinese. When we couple that with the fact that we know the Chinese government purchased missiles from the former Soviet Union, there is plenty of reason for us to show concern—perhaps even alarm.

"It all depends on what we're dealing with. A meltdown? Spilled waste? A test gone bad? What? My government believes that it is imperative that we find out."

Rebi Chernov's smile had long since faded. "And I too am alarmed, Agent Seacord. But I am alarmed because I know what radiation sickness is. I have studied what happened at Chelyabinsk where four out of every five inhabitants in the affected area still suffer severe headaches, bleeding, anemia, and even leukemia. Who knows how many may have already died or will die prematurely? When you tell me your primary concern is for the safety of Dr. Hamilton and the fact that the Chinese may have stolen technology, your reason for being here does not impress me.

"I have spent long hours studying the effects of what happened at Chernobyl. We have documented cancer, extensive damage to bone marrow, the kidneys, and the lungs. There are people in Chernobyl and the surrounding area who can no longer see, or work. . . ." Chernov's voice trailed off and she paused. She took a sip of her drink while she regained her composure. "For two people who must work together over the next several days, perhaps even weeks, we have not gotten off to a very good start, have we?"

"I guess I had that coming," Seacord admitted. "Let's start over. Okay?"

"Tell me, does Dr. Hamilton know your real identity?"

Seacord shook his head. "Negative. In all probability his reaction would be the same as yours."

"Then put your mind at ease, Agent Seacord; your ruse is safe with me. When the others are around, I will continue to call you Dr. Shell and you can call me Rebi. Is that fair enough?" She dabbed at the corners of her mouth with her napkin and reinvented her smile. "Now, I believe I heard you say you have not visited Moscow in quite some time. What would you like to do? The evening is still young."

"I was hoping you might be inclined to show me around," Seacord said.

"Then it will be my pleasure to do so, with one proviso. We do not allow our passions or our ideologies, old or new, to further subvert our friendship."

"You've got yourself a deal," Seacord agreed.

Rebi finished her drink, stood up, straightened her skirt, and somehow managed to intensify the charm. T. J. enjoyed the show.

Outside, there was falling snow, and Rebi hailed a cab. "Slavyansky Bazaar," she informed the driver. Then she looked at Seacord. "I think you will be amused."

Building 231
Washington
5-4

Chet David managed to stop Clark Barrows just outside the elevator when it reached the second floor. "Better brace yourself, Clark. Seacord's ex-wife is waiting for you in your office."

"How the hell did she get past security?"

"She was standing in the lobby when I got here at seven-thirty. I cleared her. Managed to get her into your office without too much of a scene, too."

Barrows didn't have much time to prepare himself. When he opened the door, Kat was standing with her back to the window. Before he had even managed to step into the room, she had crossed it to confront him. Her face was flushed and her hands were shaking.

Barrows started to greet her, but she cut him off. "Okay, Clark. Just what the hell is going on?" she snarled.

Barrows tried to look surprised. "What the hell is going on where?"

"Damn it, Clark, don't play games with me. Thomas isn't in the intensive care unit at Saint Francis and you know it. Now I want to know, where the hell is he?"

Barrows walked around his desk and took a seat. He was stalling. He shoved a stack of papers aside, laid his arms on his desk, and tried to keep his voice modulated. "Okay, suppose we start by you telling me why you think T. J. isn't there."

"Damn it, Clark, this is what makes me think he isn't there. A goddamn phone call came into the newsroom late last night. Listen." Kat Collins opened her purse, extracted a small Sony voice recorder, placed it on Barrows's desk, and pushed the play button.

The voice on it was raspy and muted; the caller had made an obvious attempt to disguise himself.

> "This message is for Kat Collins. Ms. Collins, we thought you might find it interesting to learn that your friends at your former husband's employer have been deceiving you. There is no Thomas Jefferson Seacord in the intensive care unit at Saint Francis Hospital. The bed that you were told is being occupied by your former husband is in fact occupied by a mannequin."

Barrows sighed, looked at Kat and then the tape player. "When did you say you received this?"

Kat Collins was impatient. "Dammit, Clark, you're stalling. But for the record, it came in sometime during the night, last night. One of the engineers took the call. The caller even instructed him to tape it and make sure I heard the exact words."

Clark Barrows sagged back in his chair and tented his fingers in front of his face. "What I'm about to tell you, Kat, goes no further then this office. Understand? T. J.'s life may depend on it. When that pipe bomb went off in his condo, it was obvious someone was trying to kill him. But the night he was roughed up in the Green Frog parking lot, it was a totally different story. That second time was only to let T. J.

know that they knew about your daughter, Lucy. What they were saying was, if he didn't cooperate, they would turn their focus on her."

It was the first time Barrows could recall Kat being speechless. "Lucy," she finally blurted. "They threatened to harm Lucy?"

"Look," Barrows assured her. "There's no need to worry. The moment we learned about it, we had one of our agents hustle her out of Key West and put her someplace where she'll be safe until we can bring this Chen Ton matter to a close."

"Where is she?" Kat demanded.

"I've already told you more than I should have," Barrows said. "Trust me, Kat; your daughter is safe. That's all I can tell you."

"Dammit, Clark, she's *my* daughter, I have a right to know."

Barrows continued to scowl and shake his head. He knew she realized he was purposely avoiding eye contact. "I'm not running this show, Kat. This show, it's the Attorney General who is calling the shots."

"At least you can tell me where Thomas is."

"Can't tell you that either, but I can assure you of one thing. He's a long way away from where Chen Ton's people can get their hands on him."

"Then tell me this. What the hell is the government waiting for? Why doesn't the Attorney General bring Chen Ton in and charge him?"

"With what? These things take time. The AG's people are building their case. This is a very convoluted matter, Kat. We're trying to avoid charging Chen with something that won't do anymore but get him sent back to China.

"The AG wants to at least hang this guy with accessory to murder. Chen has an airtight alibi for the night Bridgewater was killed. He was on the West Coast the night they bombed T. J.'s condo, and again on the night T. J. was roughed up in the parking lot. He is slippery.

"All the AG has so far is a lot of very circumstantial evidence . . . and that won't get the job done. Chen was manipulating Ben Bridgewater with campaign funds. We know that, but we can't prove it. We don't have an airtight case, at least not yet.

"We are also convinced Chen has been able to get some of his own people into some very sensitive positions in places where they can do a great deal of harm. We are trying to dig them out, but we don't have all of the names yet. The only thing we can nail Chen on at the moment won't get anything done. The AG claims that if they haul Chen in now, his lawyers would have him back on the street in a matter of hours. If we can't hold him once we bring him in, he's long gone—and if he gets back to China, there is no way to extradite him."

If Clark Barrows was unable to remember the last time Kat was hard-put for words, he was equally ready to admit he had never seen her cry. But now, for the first time, he was seeing tears. "I'm frightened, Clark," she admitted.

"Believe me, Kat, you have every right to be. For the moment, though, we've taken every precaution we know how to take."

Irkutsk
5-5

With Chenko remaining in Moscow as planned, Chernov, Hamilton, and Seacord caught the Aeroflot flight from Moscow to Irkutsk early the following morning. The flight took the better part of seven hours, and the IHO contingent was greeted by unexpectedly hostile weather upon their arrival. A hundred miles or so west of their destination, their flight began to encounter heavy turbulence, and there was an announcement by the pilot. When he was finished, Rebi interpreted.

"He said the weather has continued to deteriorate at Irkutsk. Apparently a low-pressure area has moved in, and it seems our destination is in the midst of an early winter storm. We are being told to prepare ourselves for twenty degrees Fahrenheit when we land, and that the airport is reporting winds in excess of twenty kilometers and moderate snow."

"How far will this set us back?" Hamilton questioned.

The woman shook her head as she shrugged. "The storm is a bit earlier than usual and there is no way of knowing, but I feel certain we can anticipate more of the same. If the weather holds to form, it will be quite cold and very windy in the valley of the Solonge this time of year. I do not think any of us will find it pleasurable."

Some forty-five minutes later, inside the terminal, after Rebi had maneuvered them through ground authorities, Ugan Sergee materialized. He wore a greatcoat and a fur hat, and his brooding, almost bovine appearance was not at all what Seacord had anticipated.

Ugan Sergee was multilingual. Like Rebi Chernov, his education in Switzerland and Russia had enabled him to master a number of different languages. In addition, he was fluent in a variety of Mongolian regional dialects. Seacord soon learned, however, that while he was more than comfortable with both Russian and Chinese, he was decidedly less proficient with English; when he spoke that, he had the curious habit of referring to himself in the third person.

"Dr. Chenko tells us you know the territory around the Kamanchu area as well as anyone," Rebi began. She spoke in English to avoid having to interpret for Seacord and Hamilton.

Ugan Sergee was the kind of person who talked with his hands. "Sergee is familiar," he confirmed. Then he stopped to light a cigarette. "My friend Josef was most right. From what Sergee has learned, it is quite known that there have been some sort problems at Kamanchu. What kind? Sergee unable to know. But Sergee all time asking questions. Sergee tell you this much. Whatever problem is, they do much to conceal it.

"Sergee also hears much whispers that garrison of Chinese guards being sent to Kamanchu." He paused while he finished his cigarette. In reality he was waiting for the IHO team to digest what he was saying. At the same time he was doing his best to carve a smile out of his craggy features. "Sergee's country is country of rumors. There is much whispers in capital that Americans and Russians sending people to investigate."

Hamilton looked surprised. "I am curious as to how your people know this," he said.

When Ugan Sergee smiled the second time, he revealed the fact that he had reached the stage of life in his country where he could claim very few teeth—with the exception of gold ones. The others that remained were stained and crooked. "We have but two televisions in Sergee's country, both owned by state—one Russian, one Mongolian. Most Sergee country not speak Russian. That leaves much talk time. Sergee hear plenty talk Russians and Americans talk to Sergee's government. Also talk to Chinese. Talk about what happen at Kamanchu. Much interest. When Josef call, he ask for Sergee's help. Sergee put talk pieces together. Sergee think you are here only because IHO need learn much."

Chernov and Seacord looked at each other. Seacord was smiling. "So much for sneaking up on them," he muttered. Then he looked at Hamilton. "From what Sergee tells us, they know we're coming. If that's the case, it's going to make things even more difficult."

Sergee nodded. It was obvious he understood English better than he spoke it. "Sergee made questions. Sergee learn PRK garrison security commander at Jingsan Dam, man name Kang Lim. Kang Lim make need known more troops. If true, Sergee reason for that alone there be problem. Small team of IHO not be threat. Sergee think there be another problem."

"Did Dr. Chenko inform you that the reason we are here is to see if we can determine the cause of excessive pollution along the banks of the Solonge near the Jingsan Dam?" Rebi phrased the question in Russian, and then repeated it in English to make certain Seacord and Hamilton understood.

Sergee appeared to be relieved that he did not have to go through the tortuous routine of trying to sift through his limited English vocabulary to find the right words. He replied in Russian. "Sergee's friend Josef informs me that you have pictures. Sergee is familiar with the area of which he speaks; it just beyond Jingsan Bridge."

"Then you know where to take us?" Hamilton pressed.

It was back to English, and Sergee responded with an exaggerated nod of the head. "Sergee all ready when you all ready."

"Our equipment should be here by now," Rebi explained. "I will check on it as soon as we are through here. Dr. Chenko made provisions to have everything we require shipped to Irkutsk as soon as he learned Dr. Hamilton had obtained permission for the IHO to proceed with the investigation."

"If everything checks out," Hamilton said, "then there is no reason to delay. We can go over the equipment tomorrow morning, and perhaps get a day's jump on the people at Kamanchu before they get reinforcements."

By the time they had reached the hotel and grabbed a bite to eat, it was going on eight o'clock. The winter storm Rebi had learned about earlier was now hammering the city with gale-force winds. More than six inches of snow had fallen, and conditions were made worse by the wind, which by the time they had retired to their hotel had drifted to make many of the streets impassable.

At the hotel, Rebi, gathered her three associates in her room and began going over their equipment inventory.

"I have confirmed that our equipment has arrived and appears to be in one piece," she said. "That is not always true in my country. The Russian government is supplying us with a TN4-3 truck, designed specifically for use in Siberia and other remote areas. I am told there are very few good roads in the location where we will be conducting much of our investigation. Our reconnaissance people describe the area as being connected mostly by mountain trails and goat paths. However, I can assure you the TN4-3 is more than capable of handling the terrain we expect to encounter. It has been outfitted with a temporary cargo bay located in what would normally be the personnel compartment. That will carry most of our gear.

"When we reach what we believe to be the contaminated area, it will be necessary to wear protective attire. You will find this attire to be both cumbersome and restrictive. But unless we encounter something totally unanticipated, it should afford us the protection we will need. Each of us will be equipped with a backpack containing portable LS-2 computers. The LS-2 is a multifaceted piece of gear. It will monitor life-support systems, enable us to evaluate the environmental conditions we are encountering, and assist us in conducting necessary experiments. If the LS-2 units have a shortcoming, they are heavier than desirable and therefore fatiguing.

"The protective suits we will wear are constructed

of modular body panels constructed of Kavinov, a product developed by Russian scientists. It was used extensively in our work at the Chernobyl site.

"In addition to the gear required to insure our safety, each of us will carry ample communications gear, digital cameras to record what we find, and whatever other gear each of us as individuals feel we need to accomplish our mission.

"As you look over the inventory, I think you will find that Dr. Chenko has seen to it that we are well prepared." Rebi Chernov paused, smiled, studied the faces of the three men, and added, "If what Sergee tells us is true, that the Chinese garrison guarding the Jingsan Dam has requested additional manpower, then I think it is safe to assume we can expect even more difficulty in accomplishing our mission than we originally anticipated. Quite obviously, the Chinese are concerned about what we might find."

Seacord waited, then finally looked at Hamilton. "You've had plenty of opportunity to study the data, review the photographs, and talk to your colleagues, Miles; what do you think we'll run into?"

Hamilton hedged. The situation had gotten more convoluted than he had anticipated. His smile wasn't quite as brave as it had been earlier. "I have been trying to prepare myself mentally for just about anything relating to what we would find when we finally got to Kamanchu—anything from a toxic waste spill to a reactor failure. The thing I wasn't prepared for was for our Chinese friends to openly oppose our efforts. The fact that their facility officer, Kang Lim, has requested additional manpower alarms me."

"What about you, Dr. Chernov?" Seacord asked.

Unlike Hamilton, Rebi Chernov knew what she wanted to say. "At no time did I think our task would be easy. I anticipated the weather and the worst when we arrived at the site. Because of their initial response, I also expected a decided lack of cooperation from the Chinese and Mongolian authorities. I agree with Dr. Hamilton, though. The question of how far the Chinese are willing to go to stop us from determining what went wrong at Kamanchu is worrisome."

Seacord agreed. "It's beginning to sound like we may have bitten off more than we can chew."

Chernov stiffened. "Do I detect language that indicates you and Doctor Hamilton are ready to back out?"

It was another small clash between the two, but Seacord's response was straightforward. "No, Doctor, we're not ready to back out. But I think we are justified in taking time to rethink our plan—just to make sure there aren't any holes in it that will get us killed."

Later that same night in the privacy of his Irkutsk hotel room, Seacord made his first call back to Washington. To his surprise, Vince Rubbra was on duty. The Kenyan's voice sounded like that of a computer. As usual, it gave Seacord the feeling he was talking to a machine.

"Vincent, is our line secured?"

"The computer is running line checks."

Seacord waited until Rubbra gave him the go-ahead. "We made contact with the man Dr. Chenko lined up as our guide," Seacord said. "His name is Ugan Sergee, and I'm not at all certain I like what I see. Get your head together with Chet David and see what you can dig up on this guy. See if you can locate a photograph and see if we can get any info about what he's been doing since he parted company with the GRU."

At that point Seacord hesitated, and waited for Rubbra to break the silence on the other end of the line. Before the man did, however, Seacord added, "We're at the Baikal and it's touch-and-go about how much longer we'll be here. Anything later than very early tomorrow morning local time might be too late to get back to us. As it now stands, we're due to leave here as soon as we get the equipment checked out."

"I will get back to you as soon as we know something," Rubbra confirmed.

Chapter Six

Building 231
Washington
6-1

Few things bothered Clark Barrows more than having his routine disrupted—but that was exactly the way his day had started. It had taken longer than usual to get his standard bagel and coffee at Sandersons. There had been a fender-bender on the beltway that cost him another twenty minutes. Then, just as he pulled into his parking slot by the security gate, it had started to rain. Sans umbrella, he was forced to thread his way through a maze of cars, and ended up in the lobby wet, out of breath, and disgruntled. By the time he passed through the retina scan, he had lost even more time.

The situation worsened when for the second day in a row, Chet David met him outside the elevator. He was disheveled, his eyes were puffy, his tie was loose, and his shirt was wrinkled. "Chief," he said. "I hate to hit you with this before you even get to your office—but Harry Driver just called. You've got a ten o'clock meeting with him at his office. He wants to know, and I quote, 'Where the hell are the updates on the IHO gig?' "

Clark Barrows felt like going back home and starting the day over.

Then Chet hit him with the rest of it. "And . . . we've got a problem."

Barrows opened the door to his office, set his briefcase on his desk, and turned back to his assistant. "What kind of problem?"

"T. J. reported in last night just as I was getting ready to leave. He said everything was working according to plan until they got Irkutsk. It seems that Chenko took it on himself to hire a guide for when the IHO team crossed over the border into Mongolia. The guy's name is Ugan Sergee. This is a copy of what Brownie was able to come up with over at central file." He handed Barrows the computer printout.

File: 023-04298: Access code MAG-41-cc
Ugan Sergee, DOB 51-5-5, Ht. 5' 8", Wt. 247 lbs.
P.O.B.: Ulan Bator, Mongolia
Soviet Academy at Frunze 74/5–77/8

Entitlement: Classified (code TN-88-51)
Assignment: 71-classified, 73-classified, current-classified.
Activity: Travels frequently between Ulan Bator and Beijing.
Summary statement: Despite denial, believed to be agent for PRK. No record of Party affiliation. Frequent contact with known Party consorts.

Barrows read the report a second time, looked at the attached photo, and shook his head. "He sure as hell won't win any beauty contests."

"Okay, the question is, does the summary statement bother you like it does me?"

Barrows nodded. "Were you able to get clearance to open the TN-88 files at NSC?"

"Negative. I'm still waiting. They've got some green ass on the desk over there at night. He says he has to see your voiceprint before he'll authorize opening the central file."

Barrows shook his head—Chet assumed it was dismay at how the day had started—then walked around his desk, sat down, pried the lid off his coffee, and took out the bagel. He took a bite and washed it down with a couple of quick swigs of coffee before he turned on his work station. Then he keyed in his password and gave the verbal authorization to open the file. While the Vp-o was being validated, the words SEARCH AUTHORIZED trailed across the screen on his monitor.

"Key question. How much of what you've learned so far were you able to get back to Seacord?"

"I've filed—but so far no confirmation."

Barrows took another swig of coffee. "What's our chances of getting through to him if the IHO team has already crossed over the border into Mongolia?"

"Slim to none. Rubbra doesn't like the setup either. He says Seacord is in a tight spot. He says there is no telling what would happen if the Russians caught him transmitting and found out they had a real live G7 agent tromping around the area. Rubbra seems to think that from here on out, Seacord will have a tough time getting anything out and we'll have a tough time getting anything in."

Barrows permitted himself the luxury of a deep sigh; Mary had told him that sighs were good for him. "Any other ideas?"

David shook his head. "Negative. I tried working through Chenko's office. According to Chenko they were scheduled to leave Irkutsk after they checked out their equipment. Then they were heading south to a small border village by the name of Kazan. They plan to cross the border today and try to get as close to the Kamanchu area as they could before nightfall."

"Any other time we would be delighted they were making such speedy progress," Barrows said. "Does it sound to you like they are overestimating themselves?"

"Chenko doesn't think they'll get as far as Kamanchu."

"And this guy Sergee will be leading them?"

"With Sergee leading them," David confirmed.

Barrows picked up the photograph of Ugan Sergee again and studied it for several moments. "Here we were being so damned cautious, keeping everything under wraps, and up pops the devil in the form of a former Mongolian GRU agent."

David was frowning. "The fact that T. J. hasn't responded to my last transmission makes me think the message didn't get through and they're already en route. He's probably packed his communication gear somewhere where he can't get to it."

While Clark listened, he continued to study the black and white photograph of the man Josef Chenko had selected to take the IHO team to Kamanchu. "Know something, Chet? I hope to hell T. J. is on his toes with this one. I'd hate to trust this son of a bitch in a dark alley."

His assistant turned to face him. "I'm not sure I'd trust him anywhere."

Arlington Hotel
Washington
6-2

Between the hours of seven and nine a.m., six days a week, the scene in the coffee shop of the Arlington Hotel amounted to little more than semicontrolled pandemonium. Regardless, it was this environment that provided Kat Collins with the last opportunity she would have to put some semblance of order in her day.

As usual, she had overscheduled her time. There was too much to do and not nearly enough time to do it. She had two interviews planned before she could write her column. There was a 12:30 lunch with Senator Langlor in the Capitol dining room, a hair appointment, and the taping of a public-service spot for the city's upcoming Festival of Lights.

Tomorrow, she promised herself, she would make up for it; she would sleep in.

She had just finished scanning the editorial page of the *Post* and was in the process of turning to the financial section when a shadow fell over her table. When she looked up, she saw a bland-faced little man wearing rimless glasses, sporting a Gump-like chin, and burdened with a bulging briefcase. He was staring at her. Then, before she could finish thumbing back through her mental card file for a name to put with the face, he was pulling out a chair and seating himself across the table from her. She decided he reminded her of a toad.

For Kat Collins, the encroacher's actions weren't all that unusual or even threatening. She was high-profile. As a columnist in one of the nation's leading newspapers, she was a target for autograph seekers, lobbyists, people looking for a connection, and an assortment of others too varied to profile. The autograph seekers she tried to accommodate. The rest got two minutes, maybe less, and a curt "Please go away." It was this decidedly icy side of Kat Collins that was generally enough to send the unwanted packing.

"Ms. Collins?" the man began. He had a small voice and a slight accent. She couldn't decide what kind.

Kat studied the man for several moments before she responded. "Do I know you?" It was her standard query before hauling out the ice pick.

In the Arlington Hotel coffee shop, Kat could be anything she wanted to be. This was her playground, her backyard. She had interviewed the President in a small room off the lobby once, and she had danced with the Vice President in the Arlington Ball Room. In the Arlington, she was always surrounded by people she knew, and sitting a scant two tables away were two young men from the *Post*'s marketing department. Kat Collins knew both of them; one had even worked as an intern in the editorial department the previous summer. At the first sign of trouble, the slightest nod of her head would have been all that was required to get both of them to come to her rescue.

"I doubt that you know me," the man began. "But then someone in your position is probably used to encounters with any number of people who recognize you."

Kat stiffened. There was always one—a crackpot, a hanger-on, a schemer, a someone who wanted something. It went with the territory. She turned down the thermostat. "I would appreciate it if you would say your piece, Mr. Whoever-you-are, and go away. I'm very busy."

The little man held up his hand in a halting motion. It was small and his nails were meticulously manicured; for Kat the gesture bordered on effeminate. "As a matter of fact, I have something to say, Ms. Collins. So before you dismiss me, you should know that I have in my possession a document you might be interested in. It's a survey."

"A survey?" Kat repeated. Then she laughed. She had to give him credit; it was a new approach. "Look, Mr. Whatever-your-name-is, I'm already late for an editorial meeting. If you have a survey you want me to look at—and it is legitimate—I would be happy to do so. Just mail it to my office. Obviously, if you know me, you know where I work." She worked up a small smile, doing her best to defuse the little man's intensity.

"I'm afraid it's not that kind of survey, Ms. Collins. You see, my employer is a very private individual. He has instructed me to see that no one sees these questions or overhears your responses. I can assure you, anything you tell me will be held in the strictest confidence." With each word his voice continued to soften. It had become barely audible above the din in the crowded room. Kat found herself straining to hear him. He was winning. Kat wasn't used to losing these encounters.

Finally she said, "Look, if this is a joke, I don't like it. And even if it is legitimate, I don't like the way you're approaching it. Now, for the last time, please go away before I make a scene."

The man leaned forward again with his arms folded over his briefcase. "Would you be so eager to send me away if I told you I know ways of securing your cooperation?"

"Securing my cooperation?" Kat repeated. "Either this is a joke or you're a crackpot, right?"

"Quite the contrary. No humor is intended, and I assure you, I'm quite sane. For example, the initial phase of the survey is a word-association test. How would you respond to the word 'daughter' or the name Lucy?"

Despite the crowd of people seated at tables around her, for Kat Collins the room suddenly went silent. She could hear her heart beat. "What about Lucy?"

she finally managed. Suddenly she was frightened, and her voice had a perceptible quiver.

"Please don't be alarmed, Ms. Collins. I assure you your daughter is quite safe—for the moment. She's in Boston, you know."

"How do you know that?"

"How we"—he stressed the word *we*—"know is not relevant. The fact that we do know is quite relevant. It is, shall we say, the key to the next question in our little survey."

Kat waited. Her carefully cultivated icy demeanor was no longer serving its purpose. She considered screaming.

"You see, we are really a great deal more interested in the girl's father than we are the young lady—a very pretty young thing, I might add." The man reached in his briefcase and produced a snapshot of Lucy standing on a Key West street corner. "All of us who are working on this project think she is quite attractive. Such lovely green eyes."

"You said next question, you son of a bitch."

"Where is your former husband?"

Kat Collins felt her breath catch in her throat. "I don't see what my former husband has to do with this."

"My client is most eager to learn his whereabouts."

It had taken several minutes, but Kat was finally able to regain a small degree of composure. She tried to weigh her words, hoping that when she did, she would sound convincing. "My husband and I are divorced," she began carefully. "He's in the Navy. He could be anywhere. I don't keep track of him."

For the first time since the little man had sat down,

he exhibited something akin to a thinly veiled smile. Somehow it managed to be both sardonic and malevolent at the same time. It was obvious he had seen through her lie.

"My, my, you do disappoint me, Ms. Collins. We know that you have frequent contact with your former husband. We also know that he has been affiliated with G7 for several years now. Knowing that, would you care to rethink and perhaps rephrase your response to my question?"

"I honestly don't know where he is," she repeated.

For the briefest of moments, Kat Collins thought the man believed her. Instead he leaned back in his chair, picked up his briefcase, opened it, took out a small business-card holder, and handed her his card. There was no name, no firm, no address, only a telephone number. "If your memory improves, Ms. Collins, you can call that number." Then he paused. "Perhaps I should add that I would not be acting responsibly if I did not also mention that you have just forty-eight hours to make that call. If we do not hear from you in that time, then we will be forced to search out other avenues of obtaining the information we seek. That search will begin with your daughter."

"Leave my daughter out of this," Kat snarled. She was surprised at the sudden strength in her voice.

"We will be most happy to accommodate your request, Ms. Collins. Frankly I abhor Boston this time of year. The weather can be so unpleasant." At that point he closed his briefcase and stood up. "Did I mention that if you fail to provide us with the information we are seeking and it becomes necessary to turn elsewhere, you will no longer be of use to us and you will be considered expendable?"

Before Kat could respond, the little man was gone.

Kat's hands were still shaking when she fumbled through her purse to pay her bill. Initially she had been tempted to follow the messenger, look for him, maybe even report him . . . but she knew that would serve no purpose. Report him for what?

Still distracted, still upset, she hustled through the crowded Arlington lobby, crossed the sidewalk, waited for the traffic light to change, and started to cross the street to her office at the *Post*.

In rapid sequence she rocketed through a full-featured nightmare. First she heard the warning scream, and then the piercing squeal of tires. Ultimately she felt the impact. After that, the Kafkaesque world of Kat Collins rapidly dissolved into pain and finally blackness.

Mongolian-Russian Border
6-3

From the time they left Irkutsk early that morning in the TN4, the IHO team was confronted with a cold, steady drizzle. That drizzle, coupled with the previous night's snowstorm, only made the going more difficult. From time to time the drizzle deteriorated into a stinging sleet, and when they crossed the border into Tierga the weather somehow managed to worsen.

As it turned out, the combination of foul weather and treacherous roads wasn't the only thing the IHO team had to contend with. On three different occasions after leaving Irkutsk, someone in the group had reported feeling tremors, the third of which was decidedly stronger than the first two.

Now, only minutes after crossing the border at Tierga, Sergee was put to his first test; talking to the Mongolian border guards. Seacord meanwhile found himself huddling next to the warm hood of their Russian-built TN4 in an effort to ward off the chill.

Despite the weather up until they reached Tierga, Rebi Chernov had indicated she was pleased with their progress. They had completed their equipment check earlier that morning, taken inventory, and made acceptable progress on roads where the drizzle turned the snow to slush and the slush eventually became rutted ice.

It was midafternoon when they found themselves stalled on the outskirts of a Mongolian village, stymied by Tierga border guards.

Tierga wasn't on the map, and, as it turned out, wasn't really a village either. It was nothing more than a tiny cluster of nondescript, hastily constructed two-story cinder-block buildings designed to bivouac a contingent of Mongol and PRK border guards.

Less than fifty feet from where he was standing, Seacord and Chernov watched as Hamilton and Sergee continued what had become a marathon conversation with two young Mongolian guards. The delay had already taken thirty minutes, and now, for the second time, one of the guards was stepping away, presumably to either make a phone call or check with one of his superiors.

The man had been gone for several minutes when he finally emerged from the squat gray building accompanied by a young man wearing the uniform of the Chinese PRK. He was shorter than Hamilton, taller than Sergee, and wore thick glasses. The slight hesitation in the way he approached the IHO team divulged the fact that he was not altogether certain he knew what to do or what to say.

When he finally spoke, it sounded like a mixture of Mongolian and Chinese. It was obvious to Seacord that wearing the PRK uniform and being in charge of Mongol guards had impacted how he communicated.

Sergee listened, replied several times, finally pushed his woolock back on his head and in his own butchered English, repeated fragments of the conversation for Hamilton. To Seacord it sounded as if Sergee was having difficulty converting the mixture of Mongolian and Chinese into something Hamilton could understand.

"He tell Sergee this not regular way to do it. He tell Sergee most times when official of another country cross border into his country they already have clearance. He tell Sergee we not have right papers."

"Then tell him he to check with his superiors," Hamilton bluffed. "Tell him to take another look at our passports and papers; we have all the necessary permits." Hamilton was banking on the fact the young officer had at least some knowledge of English and could pick up fragments of what he was saying. He knew he had guessed right when the officer attempted to interrupt while he was still speaking.

The PRK officer gestured with his hands. He was trying to explain to Sergee that routine communications between his post and headquarters had been disrupted now for several weeks. "Not work," he insisted. He finished by telling Sergee that Hamilton's entire entourage would have to be detained until his captain arrived later that day.

Sergee again translated, and Seacord could read Hamilton's body language as he listened. The man from IHO was growing impatient. Years spent cultivating punctilio and adhering to the rules wasn't doing him a whole lot of good at the moment. He was again holding out the papers for the PRK officer's scrutiny, but the young man was doing a good job of ignoring them.

Hamilton knew Chenko himself had arranged for the forged documents, and the Russian director had repeatedly assured him they would be more than adequate to get the group past any border disputes.

Again there was an exchange between the officer and Sergee, and again Sergee attempted to explain. "PRK tell Sergee Mongolian approval not enough, he must have approval of Captain Xin."

Hamilton appeared to be on the verge of giving up. "All right, ask him where we can find this Captain Xin?"

"PRK officer say he be here later."

Seacord had been listening at a distance. Finally he turned to Rebi. "It looks like our boy Sergee is getting nowhere fast. According to the map, if we could get started now—even allowing for roads no better than the goat trails we've been on so far—we could be more than halfway to the Solonge by nightfall."

The Russian woman hesitated several minutes before she decided to say something. "Just how good an actor are you, Dr. Shell?"

Seacord looked at her. He was scowling. "I was

sensational as a snowman in a Christmas pageant in the third grade."

"Good enough. Crawl up in the truck, lean your head back, close your eyes. Pretend to be ill."

"How ill?" Seacord quipped.

The woman smiled back at him. "The sicker, the better. A little moaning and groaning at the appropriate time could make it even more convincing."

As soon as Seacord crawled back into the cab of the TN4, Chernov moved away and approached the three men. She knew she had to be careful how she played it . . . and the way to act this out was to tone it down. The nature of both the Mongolian and Chinese cultures was such that the menfolk weren't overly fond of aggressive women. She pushed her demure button. "Mr. Sergee," she began. "Perhaps you should inform the officer that we have with us a very important Russian official who has contracted a serious illness. Time is of the essence. We must get him to Hatgal where we can arrange for a plane to fly him to medical facilities in Ulan Bator."

Hamilton was amused by the Russian's audacity.

"Perhaps," she continued, "it would help if you explained that we fear any further delay could result in the man's death." Rebi paused for effect, then added, "I feel certain that, under the circumstances, this young man does not want to be held responsible for the possible death of so important an official."

Sergee managed to stifle his inclination to smile before he turned back to the officer and repeated what Chernov had said. Hearing Sergee, the officer gradually changed his expression from defiance to uncertainty. He threaded his way between Chernov and

Hamilton and approached the truck. When Seacord heard him coming, he rolled his head to one side, squinted at the man, and moaned appropriately.

It was enough. Chernov's ruse worked. The young officer changed his mind. The thought of being responsible for the death of a Russian official apparently didn't sit well with him, and he looked at Sergee. "I will permit you to proceed the forty kilometers on to Hatgal—but I will send one of my guards with you to show you the quickest way. The roads between here and Hatgal are not good. The shaking earth has made them even worse. There are shorter but at times more difficult routes that will save you time for your sick friend. Corporal Chonge will show you the way."

Sergee informed Hamilton and Chernov of the man's decision. Then he continued to listen while the officer ordered one of his guards to crawl up on the cargo bay at the rear of the truck and help them find their way to Hatgal. He was still exhibiting a degree of distrust.

He finished by informing Sergee and Hamilton that they would not be allowed to travel further unless they returned to the border after arranging for the flight to Ulan Bator. "I will radio ahead to airport authorities and inform them of my decision. They will be expecting you."

Sergee relayed the officer's demands with what for him bordered on a smile. "He tell Sergee, we must return guard to Tierga. He also tell Sergee, Captain Xin must examine papers before we allowed to go on."

Hamilton was still grinning when he ordered his

small contingent back into the truck. "Tell him he's got himself a deal."

Less than five kilometers outside Tierga, the road to Hatgal deteriorated into little more than two boulder-littered ruts. Chernov was driving. With the Mongolian guard pointing the way, she was able to maneuver the ponderous TN4 around most of the major obstacles. Each time she made a turn, though, Sergee was forced to restudy the map.

In the few attempts at conversation the IHO team had made since leaving Tierga, they had been able to determine that the young Mongolian guard did not speak English. It was at the fourth such detour that Sergee finally signaled Chernov to stop. He leaned close to her ear, and she could smell garlic.

"This place to get rid of Mongolian guard," he whispered. "From here, road to Hatgal take us away from Solonge River."

Rebi Chernov reached down and turned off the ignition before she turned around in her seat. When she did, she was hefting a Russian-made 9mm automatic and she was pointing it directly at the soldier. "Mr. Sergee," she said. "If you please, inform our young friend here that we no longer have need of his services. Tell him to step down from the truck and, very carefully, lay his weapon on the ground."

Sergee repeated the Russian's instructions, and for the first time since leaving Tierga, Seacord sat up. He watched the young Mongolian crawl out of the truck, lay his PRK74 on the ground, and step back. He had a bewildered look on his face.

"Now, Mr. Sergee, instruct our young friend to take

off his clothes," Chernov ordered. "All of them."

Sergee did as he was told. The corporal, even with Chernov's automatic aimed at his face, hesitated for several moments before he finally began to disrobe. By the time he removed his clothes and shoes and was down to his underwear, Chernov ordered him to stop. He was standing in the persistent drizzle, shivering, with a thoroughly confused look on his face.

Sergee jumped down from the truck, picked up the PRK74 along with the man's clothing, crawled back in the truck, and looked up at the heavy overcast and then at Chernov. "He not last long no clothes."

Chernov was shaking her head. "On the contrary. I look at the same maps you do, Mr. Sergee. There are at least two settlements no more than two or three kilometers from here. Our young friend will find a way to survive if he keeps his wits about him."

"Wits won't keep him warm." Seacord grinned. "If he makes it, he'll have a difficult time trying to explain why all he is wearing is a pair of skivvies."

Chernov's expression did not change. "In my earlier days I was required to attend Arctic survival school in Manask, Dr. Shell. I managed to survive in conditions decidedly more hostile than this."

"In your skivvies?" Seacord quipped. He was smiling.

Chernov wasn't. She ignored the comment. "I am quite confident he will survive if he is resourceful."

Seacord decided he had said enough. He had long ago decided that the majority of women had a wicked streak in them when it came to men. He was certain now that Chernov was a member in good standing of the sisterhood.

Under the circumstances he wasn't all that certain the young Mongolian wouldn't have opted for being shot rather than being left in the middle of the cold nowhere with no clothes.

Chernov studied the impact of her words for several moments before she reached down and flipped the toggle switch on the ignition. Then she turned to Sergee. "Now, Mr. Sergee," she said. "Please get us pointed back in the direction of the Jingsan Bridge."

Sergee nodded, glanced at his watch, then up into the wet overcast. Finally he crawled back in the cab and pointed south.

77 Larkspur
Washington
6-4

Clark Barrows was just east of the White House near the intersection of 14th and New York when Mary Barrows was finally able to get through to him on his car phone. That was when he learned that Kat Collins had been the victim of a hit-and-run accident earlier in the day.

Despite the congestion of rush hour traffic, he drove directly from Driver's office at the White House to Kat's apartment. Mary met him in the vestibule.

"How is she?"

"At the moment she's sleeping. I talked to the doctor before they released her. Then I drove her back here to her apartment. To hear the doctor tell it, she is one lucky lady—nothing real serious. She does have a broken arm and a concussion. He says that while she doesn't look so good at the moment, the cuts and bruises are fairly superficial."

"How the hell did it happen?"

"No one seems to know for sure. I talked to a young man who works at the Post. He said he worked with Kat as an intern last year, and he saw her in the coffee shop talking to a man earlier in the morning. When she left, the young man followed her to say hello. Apparently he got to the door just as she stepped down off the curb. He said the whole thing happened so fast—the car was up the street, pulled away from the curb, darted out in the flow of traffic, headed straight for her, and hit her. But he said the thing that struck him as strange about the whole affair was that the driver acted as though he was only trying to strike a glancing blow. The witness said the same thing the doctor did. It could have been a lot worse."

"Did they get the driver?"

Mary Barrows shook her head. "No make of car, no license plate number, and apparently it happened so fast no one got a clear look at the driver."

Clark glanced at the elevator. "Is it safe to leave her alone?"

"Chet is up there with her. The police called the *Post,* someone there called Chet, and Chet called me. He drove over here when I told him I needed help and was trying to get through to you on your car phone. I'm headed for the drugstore right now to get a couple of prescriptions filled."

Moments later, in Kat's apartment, Barrows found Chet David in the kitchen pouring himself a cup of coffee. "Damn, I'm glad you're here," the younger man admitted. "Bachelors aren't cut out to be nurses. Every time Kat groans, I wonder if I should be calling 911."

Barrows laid his hat and coat on a chair and loosened his tie. "I saw my wife in the lobby. I got her version. What's yours?"

"I just got off the phone. I talked to the officer that investigated the accident. He claims they haven't come up with anything yet. He said everyone he talked to who claims they saw Kat get hit has a slightly different version of what happened."

Barrows loosened his tie, poured himself a cup of coffee, then sat down at the kitchen table. "Par for the course," he muttered. "Why the hell is it ten people can see the same damn thing happen, and if you ask them what they saw, they're going to give you ten different versions?"

Chet shook his head.

"Mary said she talked to the young man who rode in the ambulance with Kat. Apparently he knew her well enough that he followed her out of the hotel to say hello. He told Mary he saw what happened, and said he got the impression the driver was trying to scare Kat more than run her down."

Chet spooned more sugar into his coffee and stared at the results. "If that was the case, he needs practice. To me it looks like she's pretty well busted up."

"What about Kat? Has anyone been able to talk to her since it happened?"

David nodded. "Some. She was awake when I got here. But I was only able to talk to her for a few minutes. She was pretty groggy—didn't make a whole lot of sense—kept mumbling something about needing to talk to T. J.

"The one thing I did notice, though, was that for some reason she used the word 'threat' several times. Maybe it means something. Maybe it doesn't. Like I said, they had her pretty well sedated and she was fading in and out on me. No continuity at all."

"People who get run down by a car seldom have what you are calling *continuity,* Chet."

"I told you bachelors didn't make good nurses."

Barrows grunted, took a sip of coffee, and glanced at his watch. It was after seven o'clock and it had begun raining again. "Look, Chet, there's no need for you to hang around. I'll stay here with Mary, and when Kat wakes up I'll see what I can learn. Maybe she'll remember something that will help us make some sense of all this."

Tierga Guard Station
Mongolian-Russian Border
6-4

Captain Xin was furious. "Your orders were explicit," he thundered. "No foreign travelers of any kind"—he repeated the words—"*any kind,* are allowed to cross the border without my approval."

The young lieutenant continued to defend his actions. "But Captain, one of the members of the IHO group was quite ill. The others of his delegation were concerned about his welfare. They indicated that if he was not taken to Hatgal where they could make arrangements to fly him to Ulan Bator, he was in danger of dying."

"And you believed them, so you permitted them to—"

Lieutenant Ohen did not let him finish. "I saw the man. He was very sick."

"You are qualified to make such a determination?" Xin sneered. He turned his back on the young officer, walked to the other side of the room, and began pacing. "And what about Corporal Chonge?"

It was evident to Xin that Ohen still felt his action was justified. "Because of the recent rock slides in the area, I sent Corporal Chonge with them. I instructed him to help them find a way around those areas between here and Hatgal where the road is no longer passable. They agreed to return Corporal Chonge to his post as soon as they completed their arrangements in Hatgal. I stressed that it would be necessary for them to obtain your approval before they could continue."

Xin continued to roam the room with his hands behind his back. He was no longer making an effort to conceal his agitation. "They have had ample time to comply with your order, Lieutenant. Where do you suppose they are?" The question underscored Xin's disdain.

By the time Xin's tirade had begun to moderate, Ohen had given up. He had resigned himself to a reprimand. He no longer made any attempt to defend his actions or respond to his captain's charges.

Xin continued to pace, waiting several more moments before finally going to the door and opening it. He summoned two senior guards from the outer office. Neither of the men was an officer. "I am putting the two of you in charge," he said as he turned his attention to the map. "Earlier today, a team of four people, three men and a woman, passed through here. According to Lieutenant Ohen they claimed to be members of the International Health Organization. They told Lieutenant Ohen they were taking one of their members to Hatgal for medical purposes. Lieutenant Ohen instructed them to return to Tierga after they completed putting the sick man on a plane. They have had sufficient time to do so—but they have not returned. I want you to find them and return them to the post here. If they resist, remind them they do not have permission to travel in this restricted area, and if they still do not cooperate, you are at liberty to use whatever means are necessary."

Xin pointed to two different areas on the map as he continued. "Each of you will select two men from Lieutenant Ohen's guard detail to accompany you. I have reason to believe that if they are representatives of the IHO as they have indicated, you are more likely to find them in the proximity of Zijin Mountain than you are Hatgal."

The Solonge
6-5

The day had turned gray, burdened early with heavy clouds, and darkness was beginning to settle in when Sergee selected a place for the IHO team to set up camp for the night. The site was a sheltered outcropping some three hundred yards up from the river, not far off the Hatgal road, on the northern side of the Solonge.

"From this spot, Jingsan Bridge there when weather

good." Sergee was pointing. Then he added, "We near Kamanchu now."

It was Rebi Chernov, though, who decided the combination of bad weather and encroaching darkness made it impossible for them to do any serious investigating in what was left of the day. With the campsite determined, she instead devoted her energies to unloading and organizing equipment.

Hamilton, who had hoped to get in, determine the cause of the pollution, and get out, did not seem dismayed by Chernov's decision to quit early. He even volunteered to do the cooking. While Sergee helped Chernov unload gear, Seacord made certain the campsite was secure.

Then, with another ten hours before they could begin their exploration of the riverbank, Seacord had them draw cards to determine guard shifts. T. J. drew the first shift, Hamilton the second, Sergee the third, and Chernov drew the card for the dawn patrol.

It wasn't until after they had waded through Hamilton's culinary efforts that Sergee held Chernov's charts close to the fire and pointed out their proximity to the bridge and dam. "River flow north and west from dam. Dam seven, maybe eight kilometers more downriver. Road along Solonge go to Kamanchu and entrance to mountain base." Then he added, "Bad road. Better when weather good."

When Sergee finished with the charts, Chernov took over. "If, as Sergee has indicated, we are that close to the river, tomorrow morning we should be able to see the evidence of the degradation apparent in the photographs."

Seacord leaned back on his elbow. "If that's the

case and we're already in the area, how risky is it for us to go any farther without some protection?"

Rebi Chernov had a tendency to frown when she was working her way through a problem. "If conditions are as I expect them to be, it will be necessary for us to take precautions as early as tomorrow morning. We should be prepared to wear both the LS computers and the Kavinov protective gear from this point on. Until we are able to take readings and ascertain what we have, there is no way of knowing how strong the impact of the radionuclide contaminates are." Then she added, "In any case, we would be wise to take every possible precaution from here on in. Above all, remain alert. Take continuous readings when we work anywhere near the river."

When Chernov finished, it was Hamilton's turn. "Keep in mind that as we investigate the contaminated area, it will be necessary to obtain representative samples of the soil and anything else you believe shows evidence of contamination."

Seacord had been listening. "Suppose we get down there and discover the situation is even worse than we originally thought. Then what?"

"In that case, Dr. Shell, we will have to follow the river upstream until we are able to locate the source of the contamination. When we find it, it will then be necessary to determine what must be done to rectify the situation. Dr. Chenko will expect not only a complete description of what we discover, he will also expect us to have recommendations on how the condition can be best corrected."

"Weather not help." Sergee shook his head. "Sergee wonder if it be safe to go to river if weather bad."

Looking out through the entrance to Chernov's tent, Hamilton was more positive. "If the weather doesn't continue to deteriorate, we should be able to do what needs to be done and get out of here. On the other hand, if what we're looking at now turns to snow, it's going to complicate matters. And if it gets complicated . . ." His voice trailed off before he decided to add, "We could be in for a rough couple of days."

Sergee was following the conversation with his eyes even though he spent most of his time looking at Seacord. "What you think, Dr. Shell?"

"I'll worry about tomorrow when it gets here. At the moment I'm still wondering what that officer back at Tierga will do when he figures out we had no intention of returning to get his captain's blessing. Will he send some of his guards out to look for us or what?"

"It is the 'or what' that concerns me," Chernov admitted. "We know both governments are opposed to us being here. The question is, are they opposed enough to . . ."

Hamilton stretched, smiled, and looked around the tent. "On that rather thought-provoking note, I believe I will call it a day," he said. He stood up, fumed briefly about both the cold and dampness, and said, "I'm afraid you young people have more stamina than I do. In other times and under different circumstances I might well enjoy sitting here and chatting until the fire burns itself out. But my aching bones are telling me it has already been a long day. As a consequence, I believe I hear my tent calling. If I calculate right, I can grab three hours of sleep before it's my turn to stand watch."

Hamilton was smiling as he made his preparations to step out into the cold. He buttoned his parka collar tight around his throat, tugged down on his hat, crawled out from under the sheltering tarpaulin in front of Chernov's tent, and crossed the clearing to his own. Moments later, Sergee, far less eloquent about calling it a day, followed Hamilton's lead. As he stood up he looked at Seacord. "You stand watch first?" he inquired.

Seacord nodded.

Hamilton and Sergee had been gone for several minutes when Rebi stood up and pried open the small wooden crate she had been sitting on. She reached in, rearranged several pieces of gear, and finally her hand emerged with a one-liter bottle of vodka. She held it out for Seacord's inspection. "Before you go, how about a sample of Dr. Chenko's hospitality?"

Seacord was delighted. "Your Dr. Chenko is not only a good man, he is a thoughtful man as well. A little something to take the chill out of the air."

"I doubt if it will do that," she said. "But if the weather does worsen and slows our progress, this could be the one thing that makes the passing of time tolerable. Would you not agree, Agent Seacord, that this may be one of those times?"

Seacord opened the cap and poured a shot into what was left of his coffee. Rebi drank straight from the bottle.

"I have observed that what our friend Mr. Sergee says is true," she mentioned. "You say very little."

T. J. shrugged. "Sergee isn't the first to make that

observation. That's what my former wife used to tell me. Then when I did say something, she always claimed it was the wrong thing. So, somewhere back there, I finally figured out that the less I said, the better off I was. I guess you could call it conversational paranoia."

Chernov was amused. "Is that an appeal for sympathy?" She took another drink. "So there *is* something you are afraid of—revealing yourself."

"Maybe. Maybe not. The bottom line is, I just decided it was better to keep my mouth shut unless I really had something that was worth saying. There's some truth to that old bromide about a fellow being able to learn more by talking less and listening more."

Rebi Chernov continued to smile. "Like John Wayne?"

"You know about John Wayne?"

"I used to spend hours watching American movies. All Russians do. I grew up enchanted by cowboys. When I was ten I wanted a pair of cowboy boots for my birthday. When I was fourteen I wanted to marry a cowboy."

It was Seacord's turn to laugh. He finished what was left in his cup and reached for the bottle.

"Tell me about America," she said. "The America you know."

"Well, to start with, it's a big country."

"Not as big as Russia." She smiled. "In your country you have only four time zones. There was a time in Russia when we had nine." Her smile erupted into a girlish giggle before her expression sobered. "Dr. Hamilton tells me that you do not trust our guide, Mr. Sergee. Is that true?"

"I wouldn't exactly say I don't trust him. Let's just say that I don't know much about him, and when I don't know much about someone, I tend to be somewhat cautious. When I go into a situation like we're in now, I like to know as much as possible about the people I'll be working with. That way there are no surprises."

"You do not like surprises?"

"Not that kind and not in my line of work. My father always used to say surprises are like when you pick up a baby. There are four kinds, and generally speaking, three of them aren't all that pleasant."

"Your father was a wise man."

"Don't give him too much credit; it's an old Bill Cosby joke."

"This Bill Cosby of which you speak, he is the same one who sings 'White Christmas'?"

"No, you're thinking about Bing Crosby."

"American names sound very much alike," she said with a laugh.

"That's what we Americans think about your Russian names."

Rebi Chernov remained silent for several moments before she asked, "Are you a cowboy, Agent Seacord?"

Seacord looked around. "My friends call me T. J."

"Then I will rephrase my question. Are you a cowboy, T. J.?"

Seacord thought a while. "Haven't thought about it much. I guess I probably would have been if I had stayed home in Oklahoma and hadn't joined the Air Force."

Chernov leaned back and studied the dying fire.

"Someday you will have to tell me about this place you call Oklahoma," she said.

"I'll do better than that. I'll invite you out to the ranch and you can meet all kinds of cowboys."

"I would like that," she said.

Later, in his tent, as Seacord prepared to stand guard, he listened to the sound of the wind intensify and reflected on what now seemed like an all too brief conversation with the Russian woman.

He couldn't remember the last time it had happened, or even where, but a woman he'd practically just met had found a way to get inside his head. He was still replaying his conversation with Rebi when he pulled on his parka, turned off the lamp in his tent, and stepped out into the dark night.

Chapter Seven

Washington
7-1

If anyone had asked him, Clark Barrows would have described his previous night's sleep as a combination of fitful, unrewarding, and damned uncomfortable. The three-piece sofa in Kat Collins's living room had been designed and purchased more for its contribution to a decorating scheme than its comfort. Whatever else it was, Barrows had decided, it was not in the least conducive to a good night's sleep.

It had rained off and on most of the night. Twice

he had been awakened by loud peals of thunder and turned on the local weather channel to check on the progress of the storm. Each time, he had drifted off to sleep before he had learned anything. On still another occasion, he had awakened during a lull in the storm and thought it prudent to look in on the two women. His wife was asleep in a recliner strategically positioned beside Kat's bed, and Kat, still under the influence of painkillers, was also asleep.

It was even later when he heard Mary in the kitchen. He managed to cock one eye open and glance at the clock; it was almost seven-thirty, and he was usually in his office by eight. By the time he had stretched his aching muscles, apologized to his back, and worked his way into a sitting position, Mary was standing next to him holding out a cup of coffee.

"How is she?" he managed after he had corralled his senses.

"Groggy, but awake. She asked if you were here."

Barrows grunted, stood up, went into the bathroom, and emerged several moments later only to have his wife caution him, "If you feel like you must talk to her, Clark, make it quick. That girl is in no condition for one of your interrogation routines."

Barrows promised, wondering briefly how a sixty-year-old woman could get away with calling a forty-something-year-old a "girl," then opened the door to the bedroom and sucked in his breath. He had anticipated the semidark room and the shadows. He was not prepared for what the lamp on the nightstand beside the bed revealed.

"If you were . . . were a gentleman, you wouldn't . . . wouldn't stare," Kat mumbled. Her mouth was lopsided and her voice was raspy. Barrows started to apologize, but she w ed him off. "I know what . . . what you're thinking, Clark. The lady, she-she don't . . . don't look so good, right?"

Kat Collins was propped up in bed, her head and back supported by pillows. She was doing her best to sip from a cup of tea with her left hand. Her right arm was encased in a soft cast, supported by a sling. Much of her face was concealed by a charitable mask of gauze and adhesive strips. The part that wasn't covered was a colorful montage of purple and yellow. When she tried to speak, the words came out in muffled fragments, muted by the network of gauze.

"And . . . and don't bother to tell me I don't look all that bad . . . because . . . because I've already had a look . . . look in the mirror."

Barrows stood at the foot of the bed feeling like most men would in a similar situation, impotent and out of place. "Should I even ask?"

"Go ahead. I've been . . . been practicing . . . practicing what I was going to say when someone finally did."

"Okay, how are you feeling?"

"I feel like I look, Clark—like a piece of shit. My arm hurts like hell, my head is throbbing, and my face feels like it's been run . . . through a meat tenderizer. And that's just from the waist up. Think what this is going to do to my love life."

"I didn't realize that was a concern," Barrows joked. The moment he said it he wished he hadn't. It was the wrong time, wrong place, and wrong situation for one of his bumbling attempts at humor. He moved closer, sat down beside the bed, and took her hand.

"Mary said you were complaining of a bad headache in the middle of the night. Is it any better?"

"It's better," she admitted, and tried to smile. It was a valiant attempt, but the effort only made what he could see of her face look all the more asymmetrical. "I guess . . . I was lucky . . . lucky, though, huh? At least that's what . . . what . . . what the doctors and that damn cop kept telling me."

"That's what they always tell people." Barrows smiled. "But in your case it's probably true. I talked to the young man who rode to the hospital with you. He claims he witnessed the whole thing. He believes the driver did it on purpose. But he also said he thinks it looked like the man wanted to avoid doing any serious damage."

Kat picked up her hand mirror and studied her face. "I'd hate . . . hate to see . . . see what I'd look . . . look like if he had been serious." She paused to catch her breath. "I'll tell you one thing. It will . . . will be a while before I let them take any publicity shots."

Barrows squeezed her hand. "Feel strong enough to tell me what happened?"

Kat closed her eyes. "I'm not sure I know . . . know . . . what happened. I'm still . . . still trying to sift through it myself. I—I do remember that I was upset. I never did get the man's name, but when he left . . . I—I charged out of there damn well determined to . . ." Her voice trailed off and softened before it came back again. "The next thing I remember, I woke up spread . . . spread-eagled on a table and there was a goddamn circus going on around me: people poking at me and some clown trying to cut my clothes off. I—I remember screaming at her to stop, that . . . that suit she was sawing on cost me eight hundred dollars."

Clark had heard something. "Back up a minute, Kat, you said you were upset even before that. Why? And what man were you talking about?"

"I—I guess it just wasn't my—my day. I—I was having breakfast . . . breakfast in . . . in the Arlington coffee shop when this serious-looking little toad wearing rimless glasses sat down at my table. He was pure . . . pure creep. He said he wanted . . . wanted me to answer some . . . some questions in a survey he was taking. I—I told him to get lost. Then . . . then he said he knew Lucy. Not only . . . only that, he said he knew Lucy was . . . was in Boston."

Suddenly Clark Barrows was alarmed. "Did he tell you how he knew where Lucy was?" He was doing his best to make certain his voice didn't reveal just how concerned he was that anyone might know the whereabouts of Lucy Seacord.

At the same time Kat was pulling her hand away from him and exploring the bandages covering the network of cuts and bruises on her face.

"No, but he . . . he did say he was more interested in . . . in the where—whereabouts of Thomas."

"T. J.?" Barrows repeated. "He told you he wanted to know where T. J. was? Did you tell him?"

Kat put down the mirror. Despite being swathed in gauze, she could still do indignant. Bandages didn't cramp her style. "How could I?" she huffed. "I don't know myself and that's . . . that's what I told him."

"What happened next?"

"That's when it . . . it started to get ugly. He—he said I had better think twice about refusing to . . . to tell him where Thomas was because I was expendable. Then he left."

"And you went after him?"

"Big mistake," she admitted.

Barrows repeated the word *expendable* under his breath. At last, he stood up. "That's enough for now; you need to rest. I'll stop back later on my way home from the office to see how you're feeling."

He left the room and closed the door behind him. In the hallway he picked up the phone and dialed his office. "Put me through to Chet David," he said.

When David picked up the phone, Barrows launched into his spiel. "I just talked to Kat. I think I know what happened. From what she tells me, it sounds like that young man who accompanied her to the hospital was right. Whoever was driving that car had no intention of doing anything more than scaring the hell out of her.

"She says some guy sat down at her table while she was having breakfast and started talking to her about Lucy. She says he claimed he knew Lucy was in Boston. Then he went on to tell her that nothing would happen to Lucy if she cooperated and told him where T. J. was." After that, Barrows went silent. All Chet could hear was breathing.

Chet David had worked with Barrows long enough to know how his mind worked. Hesitations when he was in the middle of something simply meant that he was still trying to figure out how he was going to handle something or someone. In this case it had to do with what Kat had revealed.

When his boss had worked out a modus operandi that he thought was workable, he opened up like a floodgate. "Get a hold of Rick Norris and tell him to hop a plane to Boston so he can provide backup for Mark Garfield. Tell him I don't want Lucy Seacord out of their collective sight day or night. I want one of them with her twenty-four hours a day until we can figure out where the leak is in our department."

"You're convinced there is a leak?"

"How the hell else would this guy know?"

The Solonge River
7-2

For Seacord, the transition between deep sleep and the first indication he been thrust unprepared into a new day was always difficult. He could remember finishing his stint as guard, stumbling back into his tent, crawling into the folds of his sleeping bag, pulling the covers over his head, and spiraling into an immeasureably satisfying sleep.

During the night the weather had worsened. It had rained much of the night, sometimes heavily, and it had turned to sleet in the early morning hours. He remembered hearing the needles of ice pelt his tent. To make matters worse, the foul weather was accompanied by an ongoing succession of tremors. Admittedly, most of them had been modest in intensity, but there had been two, possibly three, that actually shook the ground at the campsite. Seacord had learned when he was attending school in California that he did not like ground that shook.

Now, with darkness still embracing their campsite, he was vaguely aware of the grinding sound of footsteps on the thin crust of ice outside his tent. He sat up, shivering, then slipped his hand under his bedroll and coiled his fingers around the handle of his Steyr. If he had guessed right and it was one of the Mongolian border patrols from Tierga, he was ready.

He was still in the process of planning his next more when he heard Rebi Chernov's voice. "Dr. Shell, are you awake?"

Seacord grunted. He had intended his response to be decidedly more affable than it sounded.

"Are you decent?"

"It's too damned cold to be indecent," he grumbled. "Come on in."

Rebi Chernov peeled back the flap to his tent entrance and peered in. There was just enough light for Seacord to see she was frowning. "We have a problem," she said flatly. "Sergee is gone and he took the truck with him. I went looking for him just before dawn when it was my turn to stand guard. I searched his tent, even went up on the ridge where the truck was supposed to be—no trace of him."

Seacord was still trying to get his thoughts organized.

"Except for the gear we unloaded and stowed in our tents last night, he took most of our supplies with him. The cargo compartment was still on the back of the truck."

Seacord stood up, tucked the automatic in his belt, pulled on his boots, stepped past his Russian colleague and out of the tent. The weather had managed to find a way to deteriorate further. The drizzle had turned to rain. The rain had turned to sleet. Now the campsite overlooking the valley of the Solonge was coated with a thin glaze of ice. "What about Hamilton? Does he know?"

Chernov shook her head. "I assume he is still asleep. I didn't check on him."

"Wake him up. Tell him we've got a problem."

Thirty minutes later, after searching the area around the campsite, Seacord joined Miles Hamilton and Rebi Chernov in her tent. While Chernov and Hamilton busied themselves taking inventory of what Sergee had left behind, Seacord had followed the TN4 tracks. The Mongolian had made it at least as far as the corrugated, potholed goat trail Sergee had indicated was the shortcut to Hatgal.

"I can't understand why one of us didn't hear him," Hamilton complained. "His tent was next to mine and the truck was parked less than thirty yards from my tent."

"Face it, Miles, you were sleeping better than you thought you would when you folded up last night," Seacord said with a sigh.

While Hamilton continued to bemoan their situation, Rebi sat with her knees tucked tight against her chest and her arms wrapped around her legs. In one hand she clutched a piece of paper containing the hastily scribbled list of their remaining supplies. In the other, she cradled their only radio; Sergee had taken the other. The difference was, in the one the Mongolian guide had left behind, the wires had been stripped out.

"The question is, what do we do now?" Hamilton said.

"The first thing we do is keep our wits about us,"

Seacord said. "We try to think like Sergee. Which way did he go? Did he head back to the border or did he think he could make it to Hatgal? My guess is he would have headed for the border. That way he could get off the hook by telling the border guards where we made camp."

Hamilton looked puzzled. "But if Dr. Chenko trusted him, why would he do this?"

"Rebi and I talked about Sergee after you left the tent last night, Miles. She knew I had questions about him. Enough so that after everyone turned in and while I was taking my shift at guard, I hid the rest of the fuel supply. Sergee would have had no way of knowing he didn't have more fuel with him until he ran out. That's when he would have discovered the spare fuel cans were no longer in the cargo area."

"How far do you think he can get?" Hamilton questioned.

"Well, we know he made it as far as the road that runs between Tierga and Hatgal; I followed the TN4 tracks that far. That truck was low on fuel when we stopped yesterday. I intended to fuel up when we got started this morning. Under the circumstances, I'd be willing to bet we'll find our truck no more than a few miles from here back toward Tierga."

Hamilton appeared to be relieved. "But we won't really know how bad the situation is until we recover the truck and see what else he sabotaged, right?"

"That's if we recover it, and if we're lucky enough to find it in one piece," Seacord cautioned. "I think it's safe to assume Sergee is taking orders from someone other than Dr. Chenko. If those orders include making certain we don't find out what's going down at Kamanchu, he won't leave anything behind that would be of use to us—and he'll make damn sure those border guards find us."

Chernov was less pessimistic. "Even if we don't recover the truck and our supplies, we can still accomplish most of what we came to do. If we conserve what I unloaded last night and ration our food and drinking water, we have enough to last us another two, perhaps even three days. We still have the tents and we have enough fuel for the generators."

Hamilton was skeptical. "Suppose we do have enough food and fuel to last us long enough to accomplish what we came to do. What then? How do we get back across the border to Kazan?"

"We'll have to hoof it," Seacord said. "And we'll have to hope to hell those border guards don't locate us first."

Chernov was still assessing the situation. "It seems rather strange that Sergee didn't bother with the rest of the survival gear."

Hamilton continued to scan Chernov's list. "What about the computers?"

"I've already checked," Chernov said. "There should be enough battery capacity to last us for a couple of days, at least long enough to determine what is going on down there."

"What about the Kavinov protective gear?" Hamilton pressed.

"There were three suits to start with; one of them is missing. It won't do Sergee much good, though, if he can't figure out how to operate the LS system."

Hamilton continued to look grim. "Which means

only two of us will be able to go into the contaminated area at any one time."

"For the time being that's enough," Seacord said. "We can work in shifts. You and Dr. Chernov can start poking around down there on the riverbanks as soon as you think it's safe to start. While you're doing that, I'll backtrack the trail toward Tierga to see if I can find Sergee and get our truck back."

"Do you think there is any hope?" Hamilton questioned.

"We won't know until we try," Seacord said.

By the time Hamilton and Chernov had suited up and were prepared for their first descent into the valley of the Solonge, the weather had gotten even worse. A thick deck of clouds had again settled over the area and was forming a ground-hugging, nearly opaque fog.

For Hamilton, who had in recent years spent much of his time tied to a desk job, the valley of the Solonge had taken on the mysterious dimensions of a Halloween world. He was both challenged and threatened at the same time; this was a world where he couldn't just take charge. He found himself depending on Rebi Chernov—younger, perhaps stronger, decidedly more athletic—to lead the way.

Twice during their descent he lost his footing and fell. Each time, because of the bulkiness of the survival gear, and the weight of the back-mounted computer, Rebi was forced to backtrack to assist him.

After the second fall, they had come to a small clearing less than two hundred feet above the river, a place where the fog was no longer able to conceal the extent of the havoc. Pine trees had been stripped of their foliage, plant life was non-existent, and the ground was littered with the carcasses of small animals and birds. Hamilton had witnessed the killing fields in Vietnam at the end of the war, but this had an ethereal, ghostly dimension all its own. From that point on, Rebi Chernov led the way. She kept a small digital camera poised and ready to feed the images directly into her back-mounted LS computer. On the wireless feed between them, Hamilton could hear her pausing frequently to record her findings.

It wasn't until they had made their way to the steepest part of the slope that they actually parted. Hamilton headed southeast along the bank. Using a small trowel, he had begun gathering and cataloging samples of vegetation and contaminated soil. Chernov proceeded north and west along the banks of the river, taking her own readings.

From the place where Hamilton had begun working his way along the bank, it had taken him less than thirty yards to start recording persistent increases in critical readings. At the ten-minute mark he called Rebi for a communications check. "If you are reading me, Dr. Chernov, I have some data values for you."

The woman's response came through with ringing clarity. "The reception is good. The recorder is on and working. Go ahead, Doctor."

Hamilton scrutinized each reading as it appeared on the handheld LCD screen. Some of the levels were alarming. It took three minutes to complete the transmission and make certain she had recorded everything. To verify, he repeated the sequence. Then he paused. "How are we doing?" he asked. Chernov was relieved. Hamilton sounded as though he was beginning to regain his equilibrium.

"It's working," she said.

Hamilton was relieved. The Russian equipment was working. He had heard too many stories of equipment failure with their "off the shelf" approach to technology. "Glad to hear it," he said. Then he added, "I am continuing southeast in the direction of the bridge."

"Can you see it yet?"

"Negative. Still too much fog. If I see anything, I'll let you know." Each time he transmitted, Hamilton looked back, trying to estimate the growing distance between them. By the time she confirmed his last transmission, she had disappeared in the fog.

As a precaution against losing any of the data, Hamilton continued to use the voice-actuated recorder on his LS to document each new set of readings. Then, as an added precaution, he repeated the figures a second time to insure that the data had been transmitted to the small receiver inside Chernov's Kavinov helmet.

Several minutes later, Hamilton, who had stopped to take readings on the decaying carcass of a small animal, noticed something lodged in the rocks at the edge of the river. It was trapped just under the surface of the water. Using the clawed end of his soil probe, he poked at the object several times before it was dislodged and floated to the surface. When he did, Hamilton stepped back to catch his breath. He had uncovered the bloated remains of a body.

He waited until he had regained his composure before he cleared the transmit switch. "I think you may want to see this, Dr. Chernov."

By the time the woman had worked her way back to him, Hamilton had used the claw end of the soil probe to drag the corpse out of the water. It had been necessary to make certain the claw was hooked in the belt or fabric because the flesh shredded away when he tried to drag the body up on shore.

The body was wearing a military uniform, or what was left of a uniform. Most of the tunic and the flesh on the upper torso had been abraded away by the action of the river. Despite what the river had done to it, what was left of the body displayed evidence of extensive trauma.

Rebi Chernov took one look at the body, knelt down in the silt at the water's edge, and examined it. The body was a pasty white, rigid and bloated. "He has been dead for quite some time," she said. "He appears to be wearing the uniform of a PRK officer—or at least what's left of it."

She studied the remains for several more minutes until she decided to reach into her auxiliary medical pack for a scalpel. With Hamilton's assistance, she cut away what remained of the uniform and cut a twelve-inch-long incision in the distended chest. She pried the ribs apart, and inspected the heart and lungs before she cut the lungs open, removed them, and laid them in the mud at the water's edge. Finally, she took out her camera and began taking photographs. "That should do it," she said as she stood up again. "Unfortunately, it doesn't tell us what we need to know."

It was Hamilton's turn. He knelt down at the water's edge and studied the cavity in the man's chest.

"Based on the color, texture, and deterioration of the organs, there is not that much evidence of radio-toxic poisoning. Certainly not enough evidence of radionuclide damage to the interior of the organs being the cause of death. Most of the damage appears to be external, and there is very little water in the lungs. My guess is that our friend here did not live long after some initial trauma. The organ damage we do see is due to prolonged exposure to contaminates."

As Hamilton's diagnosis filtered in through the receiver in Chernov's helmet, she continued to assess the corpse's injuries. She turned away, bent down a second time, and poked at the dead man's head with her gloved hand. The head lolled listlessly to one side, and the supperated flesh on the face peeled away to reveal a tormented muscle structure. Radiation burns were evident, and Chernov was nodding her head in agreement with his assessment.

"Whatever is in this river, Dr. Hamilton, it wasn't the cause of this man's death. His neck is broken and there is extensive damage to the areas around the parietal and occipital bones in the skull. My guess would be that he was subjected to some sort of severe and probably terminal blow to the head just as or shortly after being thrown into the water."

Hamilton pointed to where he had discovered the body and the direction of the Solonge's current. "Based on the way the body was lodged in the rocks and the current, it would appear that our friend here floated upriver from that direction." He pointed to the southeast in the direction where Sergee had indicated they would find the bridge.

Hamilton was shaking his head. "Based on what

we've recorded so far, it appears that the farther we go in the direction of the bridge, the more we see evidence of the contamination. I have double-checked my readings twice. They are much higher now than they were just a few hundred yards back."

"How far do you estimate it is to the bridge?" Rebi questioned.

Hamilton studied the map for several moments before he responded. "According to the chart, two kilometers, maybe less. If Sergee was right when he pointed out our position last night, it should be there, just beyond that bend you see in the river."

Seacord had been aware that for at least the last half hour that he had been working his way up and away from the river. He made a mental note to let Chernov and Hamilton know that as he moved farther away from the Solonge, there was less and less evidence of pollution.

In the two hours since he had left the campsite lugging a five-gallon fuel can, he had twice found it necessary to stop and rest and make certain he was following the tracks of the TN4. Because of the heavy rains, along with the rocks and debris left behind by the recent round of tremors, he couldn't always be certain.

At the second stop, several yards ahead of him, still headed north and obliquely back toward the border, he spotted a wide spot in what the PRK guard twenty-four hours earlier had been calling the road between Hatgal and Tierga. Seacord hunched down, did what he could to protect Chernov's charts from the persistent drizzle, and studied them. The road, for the last mile or so, had decayed into little more than a seven- or eight-foot-wide rutted trail bulldozed out of the trees. If they had covered this same stretch of road the previous day, he could not remember it. Since he couldn't recognize where he was, Seacord reasoned that it may have been a part of the road Chonge had routed them around in order to make time.

The path had been cleared in such a fashion that, as Seacord worked his way up and away from the river, it had become progressively more narrow. Now it was all but completely choked off by dense thickets of pine, birch, and boulders. If Sergee had made it this far in the fog, he had been lucky.

Still, it was at that wide spot in the trail just ahead that Seacord could hear voices . . . agitated voices. He moved deeper into the trees for cover, set the fuel can down, and began working his way through a tangle of ejuie pines to get a better vantage point. Finally, when he had worked his way to where he could see, the reason for the turmoil was obvious. He was looking down at a crude wooden bridge constructed of tree trunks spanning a ten-foot-deep gully no more than thirty feet across. At the bottom was a shale-bottomed creek covered by less than a foot of water. Seacord could see what had happened. The TN4 had slipped off the side of the bridge and landed in the creek bed at a forty-five-degree angle. Ugan Sergee hadn't been all that lucky after all.

The scenario was apparent. In his efforts to get away from the IHO campsite in the fog and darkness, Sergee had taken a few too many risks. One of which was trying to cross the bridge in the fog. The Russian version of a HMMWV and its bulky cargo bay had been too wide for the bridge and it had gone over the side.

Sergee, apparently uninjured, was sitting on the far bank of the gully with his hands hammer-locked behind his head. A skinny PRK guard in an ill-fitting uniform had an obsolete Soviet 7.62 light machine gun pointed at him. Despite the fact that Sergee looked like he had survived the accident without breaking anything, he was a long way from smiling.

Less that twenty feet from Sergee, two more PRK soldiers were involved in an animated conversation replete with occasional shouts and frequent gestures. From time to time they paused in their routine, usually just long enough to glance at either the disabled TN4 or Sergee. Finally, one of the two guards broke away, walked toward his prisoner, drew his pistol, and began shouting.

Ugan Sergee closed his eyes. Whatever the guard was threatening, it was enough to make the Mongolian guide rock forward on his knees with the palms of his hands flat against the wet ground. While Seacord didn't understand what he was saying, it seemed obvious that Sergee was pleading.

Seacord decided he had waited as long as he could. If the guard was threatening to shoot Sergee, he would have to wait. At the moment Seacord needed the Mongolian and anyone else he could recruit to help him get the TN4 out of the ditch. He pulled the Steyr 9mm automatic out of his belt, aimed, and squeezed off two quick bursts. The bullets gouged holes in the far bank of the gully just over the heads of the PRK trio, and they scrambled for cover. By the time Seacord had stepped into the clearing, the patrol had declared no contest. They were lying flat on the ground with their hands extended out in front of them.

When Sergee saw Seacord, his round-faced smile reappeared momentarily and he stood up. If a man could look relieved and apprehensive at the same time, Sergee did it. "You come to rescue Sergee, no?"

"Rescue, hell; I came for the truck. As far as I'm concerned, as soon as we get that truck back on four corners and out of this ditch, you're on your own. Your Chinese friends here can finish whatever they had in mind before I spoiled their party."

Sergee's expression changed. He was shaking his head. "No. No. Dr. Shell wrong. These not friends of Sergee." He held up his hands to show Seacord they were tied. "They capture Sergee. They threaten to shoot Sergee if he does not tell where friends hide."

"And you told them. Right?"

Sergee shook his head. "No. No. Sergee not tell anything. Dr. Chenko hire Sergee to work for IHO."

Seacord was still brandishing the Steyr. "I'm not buying it. You took off. You got caught. Back where I come from, we call that deserting—and back in Oklahoma we shoot horse thieves and deserters."

Sergee's rubbery face contorted into a solemn expression he was no doubt hoping Seacord would interpret as a look of sincerity. The words came spilling out. "Dr. Shell wrong. Sergee work for Dr. Shell. Sergee only trying to find out where border guards are. Sergee clever. Sergee know PRK on lookout for IHO when we not go back to border station."

By the time Sergee had finished blurting out his plea for Seacord's understanding, the man he was appealing to was standing less than ten feet from him.

"Save it." Seacord scowled. "Right now I need you about as bad as you need me."

"You need Sergee's help?"

"For the moment, yes. You get one more chance—a slim one. One even slightly suspicious move out of you and I pull this trigger. Got it?"

The Mongolian was doing his best to work up a smile of gratitude, but he couldn't quite pull it off.

"Start by gathering up their weapons. Then tell them to go stand by the truck. You might also mention that if any of them makes any kind of move I think looks even halfway suspicious, I'll squeeze off a few more rounds. But the difference is, the next time I won't be aiming *over* their heads."

Sergee glanced at the three soldiers sprawled in the mud halfway up the bank. They hadn't moved since hitting the ground after Seacord's original volley. "This is sign you trust Sergee. Yes?"

Seacord shook his head. "Wrong, round man. I don't trust you any farther than I can throw you. At the moment, though, you're the only way I have of communicating with these bastards. Now—tell 'em what I told you to tell 'em."

Sergee waited until Seacord untied his hands. Then he began barking out orders. The three PRK guards scrambled to their feet, obviously eager to make certain the big man with the tactical machine pistol didn't pull the trigger a second time. In no time at all, Ugan Sergee had made the transition from bullied to bully and the three PRK guards were the ones that were terrified.

"Now comes the hard part, Sergee. Line your buddies up on the other side of the truck and tell them to start pushing."

"You want push truck back on wheels?"

"That's exactly what I want."

Seacord stepped back and waited while Sergee relayed his instructions. The three Chinese guards were small in stature compared to Sergee, but they lined up against the side of the truck and began to push. The task was less difficult than Seacord had anticipated. In the end it took less than ten minutes to get the truck back on all fours. With the truck upright, Seacord walked around assessing the damage. For the most part the damage was confined to bent sheet metal, but he knew the real test would come when he tried to drive it out of the gully. He finished his inspection, instructed Sergee to crawl behind the steering wheel, and try the ignition. Seacord breathed a sigh of relief when the battered TN4 sputtered to life on the third crank.

Then, with Seacord making certain Sergee knew he was still covered, and with the three PRK guards pushing, he ordered Sergee to drive it out.

With the TN4 back on the trail pointed in the direction of the IHO campsite and the log bridge behind it, Seacord was again barking orders. "Okay, Sergee, the three stooges got here somehow. Where's their truck?"

Sergee pointed at a spot several yards up the road from the bridge in the direction of Tierga. "There," he said. "Chinese truck. Sergee think they hear Sergee coming. When they tell Sergee stop, he big surprised, make mistake, truck slip off bridge." He held up his hands to show Seacord how he lost control of the steering wheel.

"You ought to try telling the truth more often." Seacord glared. "Someday it may keep you from getting shot."

"Dr. Shell believe Sergee?"

Seacord shrugged. "Maybe. Maybe not. What do you know about trucks?"

"You tell Sergee what you want. Sergee learn."

"Take one of your Chinese buddies with you and tell him to open the hood. When he does, you start tearing out every piece of wiring you can get your hands on. If you see a wire connected to something, jerk it out. If they're still able to follow us when we pull out, it's you that gets shot, not them. Understand?"

Sergee understood, but he was more concerned about the three men that had been threatening to shoot him earlier. "What about guards?"

"I like Dr. Chernov's approach. No one gets hurt. You can tell the other two to start taking their clothes off. It'll give them something to do."

Sergee frowned. "You not shoot guards?"

"Maybe you haven't heard. When George Bush was our President he suggested we should strive to be a kinder and gentler nation. So that's what I'm doing. I'm striving."

Ugan Sergee failed to see the connection. Nevertheless, he repeated Seacord's instructions and selected one of the guards to go up the hill with him to the truck. Ten minutes later he was back with a fistful of wiring. He held the tangle of wires out for Seacord's inspection. "Sergee do good job, right?"

By the time the two guards had peeled out of their uniforms and Sergee had collected their clothing, Seacord had crawled behind the wheel of the TN4. "What about third guard?" Sergee wanted to know.

"Tell him to share what he's wearing with the other two." Seacord grinned. "If they handle it right, the worst that can happen is they'll all get pneumonia. In the meantime, you can start walking back toward the campsite."

"You want Sergee walk? Why? Sergee ride with you."

Seacord was shaking his head. "You walk, I'll drive. It'll give me time to think."

"Sergee can help Dr. Shell think. Sergee good thinker."

It was all Seacord could do to keep from smiling. "I don't think so. While you're leading us back to the campsite, I'll be busy trying to make up my mind whether or not I'm going to shoot you when we get back."

Ugan Sergee's expression ran the gamut from worry to a forced laugh. "You not shoot Sergee. Sergee your guide. American humor, no?"

Seacord nudged the barrel of the 9mm against the truck's windscreen and Sergee's smile quickly faded again. "You won't know whether I'm kidding or not until we get back to camp, will you? In the meantime I suggest you start walking."

Following their discovery of the PRK officer's body, Hamilton and Chernov had returned to camp to reseal a faulty valve on Hamilton's LS system. By noon they had completed their chore, and were again working their way south and east along the bank of the river in the hopes they would see the bridge.

Despite periodic indications that the sun was finally beginning to burn through the fog, it never happened. By mid-afternoon they were again threading their way along the Solonge at little more than a crawl. At no time did the hibernal, slate-gray world of the fog-bound river afford them more than fifteen or twenty feet of horizontal visibility.

As if the weather weren't enough, their progress was further impeded by the bulky Kavinov protective gear and the added weight of a spare battery on their back-mounted LS computers. Chernov had gambled. She was hoping to extend their exploration time by carrying a backup unit, but by the second hour she realized it was working against them. The weight of the extra battery was proving to be too much for Hamilton, and twice he had been forced to stop and rest.

"Is it the air supply?" Chernov questioned.

"I don't think so," Hamilton wheezed. "More than likely this is just one of those situations where youth will be served and age penalized." Chernov could see he was having trouble breathing, but he insisted on apologizing. "I am afraid that I find the going somewhat more difficult than I anticipated," he admitted. "But just to be on the safe side, please check the replacement valve on the air makeup unit again."

Rebi Chernov moved quickly, cautioning her colleague to remain seated while she worked her way around behind him to examine his LS unit. "Everything appears to be normal," she assured him. "All

LS K-1 and K-2 readings are well within the acceptable range."

"What about the data-retrieval system?"

"Working fine," Chernov said.

Hamilton continued to rest, waiting several more minutes before finally standing up. "Have you determined how much farther it is to the bridge?"

Rebi Chernov peered into the wall of fog, checked her watch, her POS indicator, and then the LCD readouts on her wrist-lock AUX monitor. "We have been on LSS a little more than four hours now," she calculated. Then she pointed to the POS display on her monitor. "We were here this morning"—she held the unit out for Hamilton's inspection—"and we located the body of the Chinese officer here." She pointed again. "Since we left the campsite at noon, we have been working our way south and east. If my calculations are correct, we should be able to see the bridge any moment now."

Despite Chernov's assurances that his support system was functioning properly, Hamilton could feel something happening to him. There was an unexpected fatigue in his voice and a noticeable leaden sensation in his arms and legs.

He tried to steady himself, and squinted into the wall of fog. Despite the fact that he was on his feet again, he was aware that the sensation of lethargy and inanition were still with him. He had made up his mind that if Chernov inquired again, he would tell her that he did not feel good and wished to return to the campsite. Otherwise he was determined to press on. He could see past his reflection in the woman's acrylic face shield, and it was clear she was concerned for his safety. At the same time he could also sense her eagerness to proceed. "Lead on," he finally said. "If we're that close to the bridge, I don't want to miss it."

"Are you certain?" Chernov asked. "We can turn back now and try again tomorrow."

Hamilton managed a half-muffled response that was intended to sound like an affirmative, and began walking again. Rebi Chernov fell in behind him. Hamilton was pleased that she had decided to let him lead; in so doing she could keep an eye on his LS gauges.

Thirty minutes later, after again stopping for Hamilton to rest, they stumbled into a ghostlike scene of macabre destruction. Shrouded in and partially concealed by curtains of chalky fog were the tortured, twisted girders of what once had been the mighty Jingsan Bridge. Amidst a carnage consisting of convoluted steel, massive chunks of concrete, rocks, and boulders, was the tangled wreckage of what once had been a train.

She heard Hamilton, when he first viewed the holocaust, mutter something that sounded like a prayer.

It took Chernov several minutes to inch her way closer to the scene. As she did, she tried to visually sort through the chaos. Much of the wreckage was not identifiable. Still, she thought she identified a locomotive, two, possibly three passenger cars, and a massive thirty-two-wheeled, lead-paneled containment car similar to one she had seen used at Chernobyl.

Her first inclination was to count the bodies. There

were at least thirteen, probably more. Recognition was difficult because of the way the bodies were mutilated and the decay caused by time and exposure to the elements.

The wreckage had landed at the narrowest point in the river gorge. It had come to rest in such a fashion that the river's flow was being drastically impeded. The locomotive and containment car were both lying perpendicular to the river, forming a dam, and forcing the water coming down from the Jingsan Reservoir to pool behind it. Chernov studied the flow for several minutes, and estimated that only a small portion of what would have normally been a heavy flow at this time of year was finding its way high enough on the banks to thread its way around the debris. Behind what was left of both the bridge and train, the water appeared to be much deeper.

Both Hamilton and Chernov stared at the scene, uncertain of their next move. It was several minutes before either spoke. Finally, Rebi Chernov stepped down to the water's edge and began taking photographs. "I believe we have discovered what we came for," she heard Hamilton say.

Chernov nodded. Numbed by what she was seeing, she replied in a barely audible monotone. "I recognize that long containment car," she said. "It is the kind my government built to help remove contaminated debris from the reactor site at Chernobyl."

Hamilton stepped toward the water, only to recoil when he recognized the bloated remnants of a man's leg and foot. It was floating in the brackish water pooling behind the locomotive. The foot was still booted and the boot was still intact.

"What do you think happened here?" he finally asked.

Chernov shook her head and peered up into the fog. For the most part it was still concealing the sheer walls of the ravine. "Obviously, the bridge collapsed," she said, "but what caused it?"

"Could it have been the weight of the containment car?"

Chernov continued to stare at the havoc. "I don't know," she said.

"The Swiss have been reporting earthquakes in the area," he reminded her. "Maybe the . . ."

Chernov moved away and began taking photographs. "See the loading ports on the containment car? Does it appear that some of the ports have been compromised?"

Hamilton's eyes traced along the top of the massive car until he identified the loading ports. Chernov was right. The seals were intact, but several of the ports those seals were protecting appeared to be ruptured. If that was the case, and the train had been en route to the dumping site in the Gobi, as Sergee had said it was rumored, the contents of this containment unit could well be the source of the pollution. Hamilton stepped back and waited while Chernov changed discs in the camera and continued shooting.

"It's been even worse than I imagined," Hamilton admitted.

Chernov finished, put the camera back in her auxiliary pack, checked the readings on her LS, and made certain she had recorded the values on her computer. "At this point, I think it would be unwise to proceed until we inform Dr. Shell of our findings."

Hamilton agreed as he continued to back away. He was again finding it difficult to breathe.

Building 231
Washington
7-3

Clark Barrows pushed himself away from his desk, stretched, and leaned forward, surveying the three open personnel files in front of him. "Okay." He sighed. "Let's go through it one more time. Maybe we missed something."

Chet David scooped up the files, restacked them, opened the file of Charles Tang, and read his notes. "Number one, C. R. Tang, hired less than two years ago, graduate of Kansas State, degree in mathematics, student activist on behalf of two Chinese student organizations, good performance reviews since joining agency support services. It looks to me like the reason the computer kicked his name out is because there was some question about his security clearance when we hired him. According to his file, his mother came from Taiwan and his father came from Hangzhou in Zhejiang Province. Plus there is this little item; his father was at one time a member of the Party."

"Damn near everyone in China was at one time or another," Barrows said. "That amounts to several billion Party members."

David nodded. "According to the file, his father renounced membership in the Party when he sought asylum in Taiwan."

"Anything else?" Barrows pushed.

"It says here in his P-1 file that he's a Boston Red

Sox fan"—David grinned—"but I don't think we can hold that against him."

Barrows picked up Tang's photograph, studied it briefly, and laid it back on the table. "What about this guy, Rondot Wei Kin?"

"Number two, Rondot Wei Kin, BA in political science, UCLA. Came over here on a student visa, applied for citizenship after he graduated, joined the agency three years ago. Speaks four different languages and applied for a passport to go home to visit his parents just last year. When I saw that, I had Marie Craig do a little more digging. His father is French—is or was—an expatriate and an official with some European financial institution in Guangzhou. I say *was* because apparently the reason Rondot wanted to go home was to bring his mother back to the States after his father died. Why did his name pop up on the short list? I asked Marie and she said she found something rather intriguing when she was digging around in his files. While he was a student at UCLA he made frequent visits to the PRC Consulate General in Los Angeles. And guess who was a newly appointed deputy official in the Los Angeles consulate at the time?"

"How close would I be if I guessed Chen Ton?"

"None other."

"How did we recruit Rondot?"

"It wasn't exactly a nationwide talent search, Clark. According to his P-1 and 1037, he was one of four candidates who responded to a standard GS posting at GWU."

"Security check?"

"Clean as a whistle."

"So what does our friend, Mr. Rondot, do in his spare time?"

"According to his background check, other than the contacts with the consulate in Los Angeles, there's nothing that would raise any eyebrows. He's pretty much a loner and according to what Marie was able to dig up, a computer geek. She says his supervisor claims he spends most of his time on the computer and is known to be a voracious reader. She also mentioned that he spends a lot of time in the agency library. He seems to be interested in reading everything he can about counterintelligence. Claims he wants to be a CR agent someday."

"Okay, what about Mr. Par Re Lih?"

"Korean-born, University of Georgia. Joined the agency a little over two years ago. Marie says the reason she brought him to our attention is that he is assigned to support services. Even though there is no indication he was involved in any of the strings we pulled to get Lucy Seacord out of Key West, he was on duty the day we ordered Garfield to accompany her to Boston. He could have hiked it up on his work station. The way I see it, he's the longest shot of the three. But he could have known about it . . . and he could be the one passing information on to Chen Ton."

Barrows watched Chet David close the files. "Dammit, we've got a leak somewhere." He was frowning. "Otherwise there is no way the guy who confronted Kat Collins in the Arlington could have known we had Lucy Seacord stashed away in Boston."

"Which leads to the question, if they know where

Lucy is, why haven't they made some attempt to get to her?"

"They don't want Lucy, they want T. J. When they discovered T. J. wasn't in the IC unit at Saint Francis, they went back to square one; trying to get to T. J. through Kat or Lucy." Barrows finished what was left of his coffee and grimaced. "I want all three of these guys monitored, Chet, especially Rondot. And don't make it too subtle. Maybe we can make someone nervous."

Chet David closed the files. "You've got a feeling about Rondot?"

Barrows shook his head. "No, just playing a hunch."

Chapter Eight

The Solonge
8-1

By the time darkness was beginning to settle in, the weather at the IHO campsite had gone full cycle. The early morning fog had finally burned off, subjugated by a high noon sun. By mid-afternoon the sun had again surrendered to an ominous cloud cover that was for the second time in as many days torturing the IHO team with heavy rains.

Chernov and Hamilton had returned to the campsite to discover the somewhat aberrant scene of a dinged-up TN4 and a contrite-appearing Ugan Sergee tethered to it. Both were under a protective canvas rigged up by Seacord.

By dark, they had eaten, checked over their gear, fired up the generators to charge the batteries on the LS units, and were discussing their plans for the following day.

"Dr. Hamilton and I are in agreement on the cause of the pollution," Chernov summed up. "It seems evident the rupture in the ports of the containment car are the likely cause of the problem. We also agree we have no way of knowing how much more waste material remains in the containment car, how much has already escaped, and the extent of the degradation. All of which Dr. Chenko would think significant in determining the size of the problem. If it is, as we believe, weapons-grade waste material, it is more toxic and could be decidedly more devastating than the toxicity we would expect to find in the waste from a nuclear power plant." Rebi Chernov paused and took a sip of the jasmine tea she had prepared. "Dr. Hamilton is of the opinion that we should return to Moscow and let people know what we found."

"Wait a minute," Seacord said. "All of a sudden I'm hearing something I don't like. The way I see it, we're not even half done. One of the reasons I came here was to find out what's going on inside Zijin Mountain."

"The problem is the containment car," Hamilton said. "Dr. Chernov and I witnessed that today."

Seacord was scowling. "Okay, I grant you, we know there is a nuclear waste problem. But that's all we know. There's a helluva lot we don't."

Hamilton's face flushed. "Must I remind you that we came here to deal with a pollution problem, Dr. Shell? If the Chinese are building and testing warheads at Kamanchu, that becomes a problem for the Security Council of the United Nations not the International Health Organization. Besides, Dr. Chernov shares my opinion that it appears their Zijin Mountain infrastructure has received extensive damage as the result of this accident."

Chernov had been listening. "Dr. Shell is right; we don't know the amount of damage. Extensive, maybe. Minimal, maybe. We need to find a way to verify the extent of the damage and we haven't done that yet. Finding that containment car is the first real proof that we are in fact dealing with a nuclear waste situation of some type. Up until now, I admit, there was a strong likelihood, but—"

"Do you hear what Dr. Chernov is saying?" Hamilton said to Seacord. "We know what is causing the pollution. We have what we came for."

Chernov was shaking her head. "No. I am afraid I must agree with Dr. Shell on that point. Knowing the source of the pollution is only half the answer. We must explore further . . . and that means going deeper into the contaminated area."

"Which is exactly what I intend to do," Seacord said.

Hamilton's eagerness to call the investigation to a halt was obvious. "Forgive me, Dr. Shell, but I fail to see what will be gained by further investigation or by further delay in reporting our findings. Each day the Solonge's flow continues unabated, the situation worsens. We now know the source of the pollution, and our first obligation should be to inform the Russian health authorities of our findings. Only then, when they have proof, can the Russian and American governments put pressure on Beijing to get the situation rectified."

"I can't agree," Seacord argued. "What we came here to accomplish is only half done. There is still—"

Chernov put her hand on Seacord's arm. "This arguing will get us nowhere. Under the circumstances, I think it is time, as you Americans like to say, to 'lay the cards on the table.' "

"Meaning what?" Hamilton said. His face was red.

Chernov looked at Seacord before she began. "Let's start with the fact the man you have been calling Dr. Shell is in reality a man by the name of Thomas Jefferson Seacord, a G7 agent. Mr. Seacord and I have already had our little moment of truth. You should be aware that he is not a doctor but an agent of your United States government."

Hamilton was staring back at her in disbelief.

She went on. "Mr. Seacord tells me that your government arranged to send him to Kamanchu disguised as a doctor to—as Mr. Seacord so colorfully expresses it—to keep you from getting 'bushwhacked.' "

Suddenly Hamilton was wearing the disturbed expression of a man who had been both duped and embarrassed. "G7," he repeated. Then there was a long pause. "As I recall, G7 is supposed to be part of the ISA's covert response team. Is that correct, Mr. Seacord?"

That's what it says in the handbook."

Hamilton sighed, shuffled his feet, then finally

laughed. Seacord had recognized it from the outset: Miles Hamilton may have been physically out of shape for the mission, but otherwise he was one sharp and capable individual. It was likely he even understood and appreciated the length G7 had gone to cover up their real reason for becoming involved in this joint IHO-Russian venture.

"I suppose it was inevitable," Hamilton said. "Our government doesn't like to pass up opportunities like this, does it, Mr. Seacord?" Then he looked at Chernov. "I deluded myself, Doctor. I knew there was risk if our government was involved, but I decided to take it. I was getting nowhere fast working through 'proper channels.' My colleagues told me I was opening Pandora's box when I got involved with something like the Strategic Assessment Center. I should have realized there would be strings attached—it was just too good to pass up. Am I right, Mr. Seacord?"

Seacord had heard Hamilton's kind of diatribe before. Everyone wanted help, but no one was willing to compromise for it. No one wanted to be used.

"You didn't care about the pollution," Hamilton declared accusingly. "All you care about is the fact that IHO has provided you with an excuse to get a peek into a top-secret Chinese military facility." His voice trailed off. For a moment he had sounded furious, venting his anger. Now he listened to the rain for several moments, sighed again, and looked at Seacord. "On the other hand, I am obligated to your Mr. Barrows. He was the man who made it possible for us to investigate."

Seacord waited. Hamilton was working his way through this.

Finally he looked at Chernov. "Bushwhacked, huh? I feel that I must apologize for my American colleague, Doctor. Apparently every now and then he allows some of our quaint American colloquialisms to creep into his vocabulary. But—I must admit that I am curious. How did you discover the G7 ruse when I didn't know?"

"Your American newsmagazines are available in my country too, Dr. Hamilton. I recognized his picture."

"Simple as that, huh? Well—so much for my government's ill-conceived attempts at intrigue."

Chernov was eager to ameliorate the situation as much as possible. "Mr. Seacord indicated your government was concerned that you might run into exactly the kind of trouble we find ourselves in at the moment. There was also concern that my own government, particularly the military establishment, would be less than enthused about the prospect of having an American G7 agent rummaging around so close to our facility at Kirensk even if there was trouble."

"You keep referring to trouble, Dr. Chernov. Did I miss something?" Hamilton questioned. "We now know what caused the pollution. Isn't that what we came here to find out? The way I see it, all we have to do now is load up our truck, get back across the border, and report what we discovered. In so doing we will be avoiding trouble."

It was Seacord's turn to interrupt. "I'm afraid it isn't that simple, Miles. We've had two governments tell us to keep our nose out of this affair and yet here we are. I had Sergee question those three RPK border guards before we cut them loose. They told him they aren't worried because their Colonel Kang, the facilities commander at Kamachu, has assured them additional troops are being sent to back them up. According to what Sergee found out, they seem to think their backup could be here anytime in the next twenty-four hours."

Hamilton wasn't through. "I find it curious that you would take the word of a man who has already proven himself to be untrustworthy. Why should we believe him now?"

"The way I see it, in this situation our boy Sergee has absolutely nothing to gain by lying. In fact, he appears to have a whole lot to lose. Those guards told him the captain of the border guards dispatched two patrols to look for us when we didn't return to Tierga. This time we got lucky. We found them before they found us.

"Apparently the other patrol is still out there looking for us. Either way, if they don't find us, we can count on them sending more patrols out to look for those guys I cut loose when they don't report back. Understand? Even without the reinforcements Kang is talking about, we've got problems."

"Then why don't we get out now?" Hamilton persisted.

"Miles, we aren't done yet."

"We told them we were on our way to Hatgal. Why would they look elsewhere?"

"Don't kid yourself. This Kamanchu thing must be a big deal. If it wasn't, why would they be so intent on keeping us out? I'm convinced the commander at Zijin Mountain is taking his orders direct from Beijing. His superiors have to be aware that both the Russian and American governments know something is brewing. My guess is Beijing is telling him to make damn certain he keeps everyone out of the area. Phrasing it differently, Beijing is probably telling Kang to protect the Zijin Mountain project at all costs."

"All the more reason for us to pack up and get out now," Hamilton insisted. "Someone has to know what we discovered. It won't do anyone any good if we get ourselves killed before we can report what we found."

Seacord ignored Hamilton's continued rebuttals and turned his attention to Chernov. "You said the wreckage of the train had created a temporary dam and that the water was pooling and backing up. How much?"

"There is no way of knowing," she said.

Seacord turned back to Hamilton again. "How deep would you estimate that water to be behind the wreckage?"

Hamilton thought for a minute. "Twenty feet, maybe deeper. What difference does it make?"

"And how deep is the water along the river where you found the body of that Chinese officer?"

"On an average, two, maybe three meters," Chernov estimated. "It varies. In many places, despite the murky condition of the water, we could see the bottom. That would indicate that it was quite shallow."

"Let's do a little barnyard arithmetic then," Seacord said. "We can assume that if there is no more than six to nine feet of water beyond the site of the wreck, and as much as twenty feet of water is backed up behind it—"

Chernov took over. "In less than a month the reservoir of water behind the wreckage has doubled, perhaps even tripled."

"And what happens next?" Seacord prodded.

Hamilton, despite his reluctance to become involved, was beginning to see where Seacord was headed. "If the scenario is one where the weather continues to deteriorate, more rain, more snow, coupled with what is being released from the dam—soon that wreckage can no longer contain the water. When it can no longer hold the water back, even more contaminated water rushes down the Solonge and the situation is exacerbated."

"Exactly," Seacord said. "But there is something else we have to consider. According to the satellite photos and Rebi's charts, the Chinese tunneled down and into that mountain to conceal what they were doing. What happens when that water backs up to the point where it starts flooding the complex?"

"Whatever our Chinese friends have worked so long and hard to construct would be totally incapacitated. Correct?"

Seacord was smiling. "Now you're beginning to think the way I do, Miles—and that's what the three of us are going to make happen."

Washington
8-2

Mary Barrows, aware that any sound was likely to disturb her patient, snatched up the receiver before the phone could ring a second time. She answered in a voice that was little more than a whisper. There was a pause, a frown, and Clark Barrows realized his wife was pointing an accusatory finger at him. "It's for you," she murmured. "Your office. Take it in the other room. And tell them not to call here. They'll disturb Kat."

It was the second straight night Clark Barrows had tried to sleep on Kat Collins's sofa, and he had the sore back and stiff neck to prove it. Still, he moved as quietly and with as much alacrity as he believed it was reasonable for anyone to expect from a man his age who had been subjected to such torture.

He closed the door to Kat's bedroom, then propped himself against the antique desk in the hallway. By the time he was able to get himself situated, Chet David was already into his report.

"This first one will knock you off your pegs, Chief."

Barrows waited.

"They opened up the TN-88 file on Ugan Sergee after you gave them a voiceprint. Get this. According to our records Ugan Sergee died in an automobile accident in Harbin in Heilongjiang Province some five years ago."

Barrows was stunned. "Are you certain?"

"I'm looking at two photographs, Chief. One is the photograph you and I saw the other day. The second is the one D and R faxed over when they opened the TN-88 file. There are some similarities, but they are definitely two different people."

"Then who the hell is that with Hamilton and Seacord and how do we let Seacord know?"

"There isn't a way to let him know until he gets in touch with us again. But the news isn't all bad. We lose one. We win one. How about this? Marie was combing through the archives and she found this. I'm looking at a 1988 newspaper clipping from Xiagun in Yunnan Province, and guess whose picture I see. None other than one Rondot Wei Kin. I had Marie translate. She says the article goes into great detail, describing a reception being held by the wife of a high-level Party official by the name of Qian Zhou."

"Remind me to tell Marie how much I love her," Barrows said. "Better yet, remind me to send her a dozen roses."

"Apparently this so-called reception was nothing more then a recruiting rally designed to get a handle on some of the locals that had applied for student visas to study in the States."

"Put a bow around it."

"Marie tells me the department has kept a file on this guy, Qian Zhou, for years. As it turns out, Qian Zhou and our friend Chen Ton were both in attendance at this little shindig. This gives Rondot a possible tie back to Chen Ton more than ten years ago. Couple that with Rondot's occasional visits to the Los Angeles consulate while he was at UCLA, and we're beginning to put together a pattern of continued contact."

"Anything else?"

"Nothing concrete, but I did talk to Rondot's section head earlier this afternoon. He gave Rondot a thumbs-up on his performance."

"Based on what?"

"He pretty much confirmed what we already know.

He says Rondot shows up early, works late, and is getting good performance reviews; to quote his section head, 'very conscientious. A real digger.' But he was curious why were checking up on one of his people. I told him it was just a routine file audit. I think he bought it."

Despite a night of tossing and turning on Kat's sofa, Clark Barrows was starting to feel better about the day. "Good. What about his current assignment?"

"For the last two months he has been assigned to support services for field personnel."

"That could mean damn near anything; support services covers a helluva lot of ground. Find out precisely what kind of information he has access to and what he has been working on."

"I'm already on it," David said. "But the minute I tell IS to start monitoring this kid, Chief, every section head in support services will circle their wagons. People are goosey as hell these days after the Hawkins affair. If this guy Rondot is even halfway alert, it won't be long until he realizes someone is looking over his shoulder. And if it turns out that he is Chen Ton's mole, he'll most likely be instructed to crawl into the shadows for the duration."

Barrows was weighing his options. "You're right. Maybe we should keep IS out of it. Let's take a different approach. Talk to Pete Grimsley, tell him we want a monitor put on some of his work stations. Just make sure Rondot's station is one of them. If he asks why, tell him we have reason to believe one of our Code D vendors is duplicate-billing two separate sections for the same service. Tell him we want to run a check. If Grimsley seems the least bit hesitant and it looks like he thinks we might be running a quality audit on some of his people, tell him you've got your tit in a wringer and he'll be doing you a favor."

"Think he'll buy it?"

"It can't hurt to try."

"If he doesn't buy it, what then?"

"Try something novel . . . like the truth. Every now and then it works."

Chet David's abbreviated confirmation that he was on it and the click in the receiver occurred almost simultaneously. Barrows settled the receiver back in its cradle, opened the door, and peered back into Kat's bedroom. The room, with the drapes closed and the lights off, was still quiet.

"She never even stirred," Mary assured him.

Solonge River
8-3

On the morning of the second day it was decided that Hamilton, still feeling a bit under the weather, would stay behind to see if he could regain his equilibrium. Seacord handed him a 9mm Uzi and showed him how to aim and fire it. "If you need it, use it. The lock is off. All you have to do is start squeezing the trigger. You'll hit something."

Hamilton shook his head. "I don't know if I have it in me to kill another man," he complained.

"It isn't necessary to kill a man to stop him," Seacord explained. "Just aim at their crotch when you start pointing that thing. If they see where you have it pointed, they'll think you're one mean son of a bitch."

Even with a loaded Uzi, Hamilton was still apprehensive. "Do you think they still have patrols out looking for us?"

"Hard to say. It seems like they would have found us by now if they were making even a half-assed effort. We're too damn close to the road for them not to find us. The fact that they haven't makes me think they may be keeping busy trying to stay out of this weather."

When he heard that, Hamilton seemed to be mollified. He pulled his blankets up to ward off the chill, laid his head back, and tried to rest.

Thirty minutes later, with Sergee still pleading innocence at every opportunity, Chernov, Seacord, and Sergee headed south and east along the high ridge overlooking the river. Chernov had decided they could cover more ground and get closer to the entrance to the Zijin Mountain complex if they drove the TN4 and weren't encumbered by the bulky Kavinov suits until it was absolutely necessary. She had detached the monitor from her Kavinov suit and propped it against the dash of the TN4. The plan was simple. If the readings exceeded the safe range, they would stop and put on their gear.

Between the necessity to take a stint at standing guard and the unrest caused by the weather, sleep had come at a premium for everyone in the group. Their second night camped high above the Solonge had been punctuated by frequent tremors or aftershocks; Seacord wasn't sure which was which. Whatever they were, they had been unnerving. When the group awoke, Chernov informed them she been awake during the most recent cluster just before dawn. She was convinced that they were the strongest they had experienced since their arrival.

By daylight, the heavy rains had again subsided to a steady drizzle. But without the wind-driven downpour, the fog had again become a factor. That was the reason Sergee, riding next to the gun mount on the front of the TN4 as a lookout, began complaining about the visibility. He repeatedly cautioned that if the fog continued to worsen at the rate it had for the past thirty minutes, it would be difficult to find their way back to the campsite.

It was only after Chernov had slowed the TN4 to a near crawl that she saw Sergee incline his head to one side and hold up his hand. When he did, Chernov stopped and turned off the ignition.

"Sergee think he hear sheep," the Mongolian mumbled.

"Sheep?" Seacord repeated. Then he heard the bleating sound as well. He looked at Chernov. "What the hell would sheep be doing around here? According to the charts, there aren't any villages near here."

Sergee made a sweeping motion with his hand while he pointed with the other. "No village. Shepherds. Many in hills. Sergee countrymen." The Mongolian was shivering, but doing his best to manufacture one of his crooked smiles.

Before Seacord could respond, Chernov was indicating she had spotted something in the distance. "Up there." She was pointing away from the river.

"You want Sergee take look?"

Seacord shook his head, "No way. Any scouting that needs to be done, I'll do it. In the meantime, don't get any ideas; Dr. Chernov has you covered."

Sergee looked hurt.

Seacord moved away from the TN4, pulled the 9mm Steyr out of his belt, and began working his way up the hill. Less than forty yards from the truck, in the direction Chernov had pointed, the outline of a small cabin was beginning to materialize. By the time he had moved ten yards closer he realized there was someone standing in front of the cabin. It was a woman, she was holding a shotgun, and she was pointing it at him.

Seacord stopped, tucked the automatic back in his belt, held his arms out to his sides, and shouted back down the hill. "All right, Sergee, get up here. This is where you prove whose side you're really on."

It took Sergee less then ten minutes to sort through the woman's fragmented story. Her name was Reanna, she had two children, a boy eight, a girl six, and her husband, Abjoe, had recently died. The woman pointed to a fresh grave site a few yards from the cabin when she described how he had died.

Sergee did the interpreting, explaining that the woman's husband had been dead less than "one moon" and that she was still in mourning.

"She tell Sergee husband just back from summer pastures. She say he talk about night earth shook and how herd grazed black grasses along the river and drank the water. She say he tell her many sheep die. She say when she wake up next morning, husband too was dead."

"Ask her when that happened," Chernov said.

"Woman say one moon. Sergee think she mean one month."

Seacord moved closer. "Ask her if she has seen any Chinese patrols in the last couple of days?"

Sergee translated the question, and the woman nodded.

"Ask her when and how many soldiers she counted."

Sergee continued his interrogation. Finally he turned back to Seacord. "Woman tell Sergee Chinese soldiers in truck pass here this morning. They tell woman they look for three man, one woman."

"Ask her how many were in the patrol?"

Sergee translated Seacord's question. When the woman responded, he held up three fingers. "Like other patrol," Sergee said.

Seacord continued to press. He wanted to know which way the soldiers were headed when they left. Sergee relayed the question, and the woman pointed down the hill into the wall of fog. "She tell Sergee she think they go road along river."

"Ask her if she knows how we can get to the village?"

Once again the Mongolian woman and Sergee engaged in an animated exchange before Sergee finally turned to Seacord to explain. "Woman say from here only one way to village: road by river. She say husband sometime work in hole at Kamanchu when rain and snow season come."

Hole? Seacord repeated the word. "Ask her just exactly where this *hole* is." Sergee translated the question, and the woman pointed to the south and east.

"Woman say big hole in mountain where many men go."

Seacord had heard enough. He worked his way back down the hill, crawled back in the truck, and motioned for Chernov and Sergee to gather around him. "Okay, let's see if we can put the pieces together." He turned to Chernov. "Back at the camp you and Hamilton indicated the water had dammed up behind the location of the wreckage. That leads me to question number one: Did you and Hamilton check to see how far the water had backed up?"

Rebi Chernov shook her head. "We could not investigate further because Dr. Hamilton was not feeling well."

"All right, question number two: Based on your photos and charts, do you think there is any chance the contaminated water has backed up to the point that it has started to spill over into this thing the woman called a *hole?*"

This time Chernov smiled. "Hole meaning entrance to Zijin Mountain?"

Seacord nodded.

"Dr. Hamilton and I both believe there is a strong probability that at least some of the contaminated water has already started to bleed back and work its way down into the mountain facility. That would not be the case, of course, if the Chinese have the means to close off the entrance. But in the reconnaissance photos there is nothing to indicate such a mechanism."

Seacord listened, nodded in understanding, and began to pull on his Kavinov protective gear. As he pulled the straps over his shoulders and slipped into the harness for the back-mounted LS computer, he opened the COM-V line and began testing it. At the same time Chernov was helping Sergee with his gear and showing him how to adjust his comp air and secure the connections on his support system.

When the three were finished, Seacord crawled back in the cab and signaled for Sergee and Chernov to follow. As she did, he winked at Chernov. "Still want to be a cowboy?"

"Is this the part where the sheriff and the posse ride in to save the town?" She smiled.

"This is it." Seacord grinned. "Hold on."

With Seacord driving, Sergee straddling the gun mount as a lookout, and Chernov monitoring the computers, they had systematically begun working their way through the fog down the rutted hill road toward the river. Some fifteen minutes later, after Seacord had successfully negotiated his way through a maze of boulders, Chernov put her hand out and signaled him to stop. She held her index finger against her face shield and pointed to the monitor screen. Seacord looked and saw it, a blinking yellow light against a gray distance scale.

"Any idea what that could be?" Seacord whispered.

Chernov kept her voice low. "I don't know. From its size, it appears to be rather large."

Seacord wiped his hand across his visor. "Straight ahead of us? How far?"

Chernov peered into the fog and counted the pulse on her handheld phaser. The only thing she could be certain of was the distance. They were more than halfway down the incline to the river road, the fog was thicker, and the signal appeared to be stronger.

Despite the regulators on the LS system, the near-gelatinous thick fog was causing a residual condensation on Chernov's quarter-inch-thick acrylic face mask. As Seacord looked at her, he realized he was no longer able to make out some of her facial features.

"Check your air gauge," he warned. "It looks like your makeup air system might have developed a minor leak. Play it safe, stay here while Sergee and I go down and have a look."

Chernov nodded and pointed at the readings on her monitor. There was a voice-actuated warning: *Advise Caution.* She checked her gauges. "Can you hear me, Seacord?"

"Loud and clear. What's up?"

"The heat-sensing grid is now confirming the location of that anomaly we picked up a few minutes ago."

"Location?"

"Straight ahead, twelve meters."

At the same time Sergee was climbing down from his platform at the front of the truck and pointing to his monitor. He had spotted the same aberration on his screen.

"Got it," Seacord confirmed. "We're getting some disparity." He looked back at Chernov. "You're a helluva lot more familiar with this equipment then I am. What kind of a profile is that?"

"It's metal," she informed him. "And there's some indication of heat radiation." She adjusted the scale. "It appears to be straight ahead."

"Can you hear anything?"

Chernov changed from the eco-monitoring mode to audio, and studied it for several moments. "Negative, but there is a declining heat ambient in all directions from the source."

"Then the target is the source?"

"In all probability."

Seacord took out his Steyr 9mm, checked the clip, released the safety, and began inching his way toward the target on Chernov's monitor. "Keeping an eye on Sergee?" he whispered. "I've lost him. Between the condensation on my face shield and the damn fog, I can't see five feet in front of me."

"You're doing fine. It should be right in front of you."

"Keep me pointed in the right direction."

"Stay left," she advised. "You look like you're drifting right. It should be just ahead of you."

Seacord kept the cocked 9mm in one hand and reached out with his other. Chernov heard him laugh. "I think I just found our anomaly," he said. "Back in Oklahoma we call these things flatbed trucks."

"A truck?" Chernov repeated.

"Maybe it's the one that woman was telling us about, with that patrol that was looking for us."

"If that's the case, keep your eyes open for the guards."

Seacord walked around to the driver's side and peered into the cab. It was empty. "You still with me?"

"I'm getting every word. If you touch it, don't take your gloves off. If the radiation is as strong as the gauge is indicating, you'll have severe blistering on any exposed skin within hours. Use the thermal probe. I can record it here."

Seacord watched the probe's color change from silver to blue.

"Got it," she confirmed. "Now, use your scanner.

I'm getting another reading—three separate targets this time—thirteen degrees, twenty meters; sixteen degrees, twenty-five meters; and the other one is off the scale. Let's say twenty degrees. This one appears to be very close to the water."

"Any idea what they are?"

"Nyet."

"Don't go Russian on me, I'm having enough trouble with the receiver in this damn helmet. It's phasing in and out on me."

Chernov ignored the complaint. "No," she said. "Now, walk straight ahead. You are no more than four or five meters from the closest one."

"I hear water."

"You're close to the river."

For the next several minutes, all Rebi Chernov could hear through the receiver was the sound of Seacord's labored breathing. Finally his voice muscled through. "I found our anomaly," he said. "It's one of the guards. He's dead. Not wearing any kind of protective gear. The body is half in, half out of the water. It looks like he might have been trying to drink some river water."

"Probably because his throat was blistering," Chernov said. "If you can, roll him over on his back, pry his mouth open, and see if you can get some photographs that convey the magnitude of the trauma."

"Do what?" Seacord complained.

"If you want me to, I'll come down and do it. Be sure to use the flash."

Seacord grumbled, hesitated, fumbled in his auxiliary pack until he found his camera, reached down, pried the man's mouth open with one hand, bent over the body, and aimed. He triggered the shutter mechanism three times and each time, out of the corner of his eye, caught a glimpse of the ghostly images created by the combination of camera flash and fog.

"What does it look like?" Chernov questioned.

"You tell me when you see the pictures," he said.

Seacord heard her laugh.

"What about the other two?" he asked. "Think it's necessary to find them and get pictures? My guess is they probably look about the same as the one I just took pictures of."

"One should be enough."

Seacord continued to scan the readings on his hand-held monitor, surfing from the values on the LS scales to the heat sensors and radiation readings. "If there is anything else alive down here, I sure as hell can't find it."

"The fog is working against us," Chernov said. "I don't think we can accomplish much more today. Let's head back to camp."

Center for Strategic Assessment
8-4

While Gerald Reimers waited for his gum-popping waitress to ring up his total, he scanned the commissary lunchroom looking for a friendly face. Across the room, by the window, he spotted Conrad Baxter.

He crossed the room and set his tray down on the table next to his CO. "Would you mind, sir?"

Baxter looked up. "Not at all, Gerry, have a seat."

Reimers cleared his tray, set it aside, commented on the sparseness of the serving, and took a sip of coffee. "So how's the adjustment to life in the big city going, Colonel? Find an apartment yet?"

Baxter shook his head. "Not yet. I'm seriously thinking about sending an SOS to all my friends. I think I'll word it. 'Help, I'm being held captive in a BOQ.' "

Reimers laughed. "I know what you're going through, sir. It took Marlene and me six months to find a place when we were transferred to Washington two years ago."

Baxter leaned back in his chair and began stacking his dishes. "Even a two-room efficiency would work until I could find something better—but even those are hard to find and, when you do find one, they're overpriced."

Reimers nodded, momentarily lost in assessing the lack of appeal in his tuna casserole. "So how's the job going?" he asked. "Starting to get the hang of things?"

"I have a feeling there will always be something new," Baxter said.

Reimers arched his eyebrows. "Speaking of something new, whatever happened to that situation with the people at the International Health Organization? You know, the one where some Russian doctor was concerned about the amount of environmental degradation resulting from a pollution leak?"

"Funny you should ask, Gerry, because I have a note on my calendar to call Clark Barrows and follow up. Last I heard, they had pretty well decided to send one of their men in with the IHO team to see what they could learn."

Reimers shoved the casserole aside and leaned forward to reach for the coffee creamer. "Any possibility they might still be there?"

"I suppose, why?"

Reimers seemed to be hedging. "Well, sir, after we had that meeting with the G7 people and I knew they were involved in the situation, I more or less put it on the back burner. I did tell Lieutenant Parker to keep an eye on it and keep me advised if she saw anything unusual. Apparently she did. When I came in this morning, I found a number of satellite photos on my desk with a note from her."

"I assume she saw something unusual then?"

"Not exactly unusual, sir, but she did call my attention to the fact that it has been an extremely wet winter over there so far."

"Lots of snow?"

"Not snow, sir, rain—they are having a mild winter and lots of rain. There has been a massive low-pressure area sitting over the region for quite some time now, and it's been dumping more than the usual amount of moisture on the area."

The expression on Baxter's face failed to reflect alarm. Reimers thought he either didn't understand the situation or didn't think it important. Finally Baxter said, "I don't think that IHO team, if they're still over there, will mind a little rain, Captain."

"The rain is a secondary problem, Colonel. It's the Jingsan Dam that may be the real problem."

Baxter scowled. "What kind of problem?"

"The Jingsan Dam is a hydrofill dam, Colonel. I'm oversimplifying, but it's primarily a big mountain of dirt and not much else. There is a lot less engineering in an earthen dam. In principle it's the same, but in reality it's a lot different than the gigantic concrete structures we tend to think of—"

"Why should it be a problem?" Baxter cut in. "As I recall, we have several hydrofill dams in this country."

"We didn't build them where there was a high frequency of earthquakes, Colonel."

"Wait a minute. Are we talking about earthquakes or nuclear tests?"

"The Swiss Seismological people continue to report a series of aftershocks in that area, Colonel. I thought you knew. Just this morning I had the opportunity to compare some of our latest satellite photos with the ones we previously assessed."

"And?"

"The combination of heavy rain and the continuing series of aftershocks following the nuclear test and subsequent earthquake reported by the Swiss nearly a month ago have resulted in noticeable erosion to the dam."

"How noticeable? Noticeable enough to be serious?"

Reimers pushed himself back from the table. "I'm not the one to ask, Colonel." He was smiling. "That's out of my area of expertise. I just don't know enough about it. On the other hand, from a novice's point of view, I think I already see enough evidence of structural compromise to be concerned. If the heavy rains continue or they experience another earthquake in the area . . . that IHO team could have a helluva problem, especially if that dam gives out."

Red Rain

Warehouse District
Washington
8-5

Rondot Wei Kin pulled his collar tight against the raw night air and continued to shiver. He had followed Chow Pin's instructions to the letter. The directions were explicit. He had been told to drive to the abandoned Hanford Manufacturing warehouse on Clay Street, park on the east side of the building, enter through the service door, and use the freight elevator to get to the second floor. Above all, he had been cautioned, make certain he was not followed.

Now, after parking, he had waited in his car for nearly ten minutes. Two cars had passed, but there were no other signs of traffic. Convinced that he had not been followed, he stepped out of his car, crossed the street, and went around to the alley service door.

For Rondot, an abandoned warehouse seemed like a curious place to meet his contact. Previous Council contacts with Chow had always been accomplished in one of the numerous Chinese restaurants in the city; never the same one twice in succession. Chow was far too cautious to permit something like that.

As Rondot waited, he continued to shiver. Each time he heard a noise he thought it would be the arrival of his contact. As usual, though, Chow was late.

There was no one to whom Rondot Wei Kin could complain about his contact's punctuality. Anyone else would have considered Chow's lack of promptness little more than a minor irritation. On the other hand, there was always the possibility it was not a flaw at all, that it was merely a man of importance being extremely cautious. Rondot knew Chow was the type who would make doubly certain that neither he nor Rondot had been followed.

Now, just as Rondot was starting to become concerned and wonder if there was something in the instructions he had misinterpreted, Chow emerged from the shadows. For a man twice the size of Rondot, the courier moved with the stealth of a cat.

"You indicated that you were concerned?" Chow began. "What is the reason for this concern?" Like most of Chen Ton's people, the courier spoke impeccable English. He was so adept at it that there was no indication that English was the courier's second language.

"I am concerned," Rondot admitted. "It would appear that someone in my department is being monitored. I fear that it is me they are watching."

"Explain," Chow insisted.

"There are indications that the files in my computer have been opened in my absence. As a precaution against such an invasion, I developed a seven-digit pass lock. It would appear that it has been compromised."

Chow's expression remained taciturn. "I trust there is nothing in those files that would betray you."

"I can assure you I have been most prudent. After I informed you that I had learned Agent Seacord's daughter was hiding in Boston, I purged my files just to be certain. I deleted all files that would indicate I had obtained the code that allowed me to investigate Agent Garfield's files and learn of his whereabouts."